I0452260

ALL THE PRETTY GIRLS

DEANNA LYNN SLETTEN

All The Pretty Girls
A Rachel Emery Novel
Book Three

Copyright 2023 © Deanna Lynn Sletten

This is a work of fiction. Names, characters, places, and incidents are either the product of the author's imagination or are used fictitiously, and any resemblance to any actual persons, living or dead, events, or locales is entirely coincidental.

All rights reserved.

No part of this book may be reproduced, or stored in a retrieval system, or transmitted in any form or by any means, electronic, mechanical, photocopying, recording, or otherwise, without the express written permission of the author.

ISBN–13: 978-1-941212-72-1

Cover Design: Deborah Bradseth of DB Cover Design

Novels by

Deanna Lynn Sletten

WOMEN'S FICTION

The Christmas Charm
The Secrets We Carry
The Ones We Leave Behind
The Women of Great Heron Lake
Miss Etta
Night Music
One Wrong Turn
Finding Libbie
Maggie's Turn
Summer of the Loon
Memories
Widow, Virgin, Whore

MURDER/MYSTERY

Rachel Emery Series
The Truth About Rachel
Death Becomes You
All the Pretty Girls

ROMANCE

Destination Wedding
Sara's Promise

Lake Harriet Series
Under the Apple Blossoms
Chasing Bailey
As the Snow Fell
Walking Sam

Kiss a Cowboy Series
Kiss a Cowboy
A Kiss for Colt
Kissing Carly

YOUNG ADULT

Outlaw Heroes

ALL THE
PRETTY
GIRLS

CHAPTER ONE

Rachel Emery listened to the evening news as she prepared dinner. It was a beautiful March evening, and she and her boyfriend, Avery Turley, had just spent a lovely day hiking near a local lake. But as she prepared the steak for the grill, Rachel shook her head in disgust over the news. Another murder victim had been found.

"Melanie Lopez, age twenty-one, a junior at Florida State University, has been found in a field near her apartment building nine days after she'd been reported missing," the reporter on TV stated. "That same field had been searched three days ago, leaving authorities to believe her body was placed there over the last seventy-two hours. We'll have more information as the investigation continues."

"What's wrong?" Avery asked as he walked inside the kitchen from the patio. "Don't the steaks look good?"

Rachel's shoulder-length brown hair swayed gently as she shook her head again. "They found the body of another young woman," she told him. "She was twenty-one and a junior at FSU. They found her in a field near the apartment she shared with another college student." Rachel sighed. "So many young women being taken and killed, and they haven't a clue who's doing it."

Avery walked over and wrapped his arms around her. "It's frustrating. Those poor girls. The state police and FBI are working on it, but there aren't any hard clues. They disappear and then show up again, dead."

Rachel frowned.

"I know you're worried about Jules," Avery said. "But she lives in a gated apartment building, and she's smart. I'm sure she and her roommate will be fine."

Rachel nodded, but she didn't completely believe it. The other young women had just been going about their daily lives when they'd been abducted. Even smart girls who were careful could become victims.

"I wish you weren't leaving for so long," Rachel said. "But I know you have to go. And it's an honor being invited to lead the investigation. But I'd feel safer if you were closer." Avery worked for the FBI on homicides and cold cases. He'd been invited to take over a task force in Idaho that was investigating a prolific serial killer.

"The case is an interesting one," he said as he pulled plates and bowls down from the cupboard. "It took a long time to figure out they had a serial killer in their midst."

Rachel's brows rose. "You mean more interesting than my case was?" she teased. They had met two years before while Rachel was trying to figure out why she'd been considered dead in her hometown since she was a child. Avery had been trying to solve the case of multiple rapes and murders from decades before. Together, they'd solved both cases and had grown close.

He grinned. "No case will ever be as interesting as that one."

She smiled at him. He looked just as handsome as he had when they'd met. His brown wavy hair fell perfectly into place, and his brown eyes were warm and inviting. Meeting him after having been alone for years after her husband's death was the best thing that had happened to Rachel.

Avery took the steaks outside, and Rachel finished the pasta salad and set the plates on the counter where they'd eat. Even though Avery lived and worked in Baltimore, Maryland, he tried to come to Rachel's Tallahassee home often. She'd lived in this home since before her husband died in a terrible car accident and raised her daughter Jules there. Now, Jules was a junior at Florida State University.

Avery came back inside. "Isn't spring break next week?" he asked. "Maybe you could talk Jules into coming to the house for the week."

"I've already tried that," Rachel said. "She's not leaving town for break but wants to be around her friends and enjoy it. Amber is heading to her parents' house in Atlanta for the week. So, it will be just Jules in the apartment."

"I'm sure she'll be fine," he said. "If this person is a serial killer, he might lie low until the next semester starts."

Rachel rolled her eyes. "Oh, that makes me feel better."

Avery laughed. "Just relax and enjoy our last night together. I might be in Idaho for three or four months. I'll miss you."

She walked over and hugged Avery. "I'll miss you, too."

They ate a delicious dinner and then watched a movie on Netflix. Afterward, they snuggled in bed, enjoying their last night together.

Sunday morning, they were both up early, and Rachel drove Avery to the airport to catch his plane.

"I'll call you when I get there," Avery said, giving Rachel

one last hug. "And don't worry about Jules. She'll be fine."

"I can't promise I won't worry," she said, smiling. "But you work hard and find that serial killer in Idaho. Everyone there will sleep easier then."

He kissed her and then went through security and disappeared on the other side.

Sighing, Rachel walked out to the parking lot. She was happy they'd had a chance to spend the weekend together before he'd left. But now, she had to get back to reality.

On her way home, she stopped at the memory care center where her Aunt Julie—it was still hard to think of her as her mother—lived. Two years before, Rachel had discovered Julie was her birth mother while investigating the mystery of her supposed death. Julie was the sister of the woman who'd raised Rachel, and even though Rachel had lived with Julie and her uncle since the age of eight, she'd never known they were her real parents. Now, even with that knowledge, and even though she loved Julie dearly, it still felt strange to call her mom.

Rachel waved to the receptionist as she walked inside the main building, then turned left and walked down the long hallway to Julie's room. It was always heartbreaking visiting Julie now that she no longer remembered who Rachel was. She'd been showing signs of dementia for a few years before Rachel had to find her a place that could take care of her. And now, Julie was fading faster than Rachel had thought possible. Taking a breath to brace herself, Rachel reached for the handle of Julie's door and opened it.

"Aunt Julie," she said softly as she entered the room. Julie wasn't sitting on the sofa watching television as she used to do, so Rachel stepped into her small bedroom. "Aunt Julie?" The shades had been pulled halfway down to block the bright sunshine from coming into the room. Julie was lying in bed under the covers, her eyes open, staring at the ceiling. She'd become so thin; Rachel was startled at how small she looked under the blanket.

"Are you awake?" Rachel asked, walking up to the side of the bed. There was no movement, not even a blink, to show that she acknowledged Rachel's presence.

Rachel's heart dropped. She'd known Julie was fading, but she'd hoped her aunt would have been better today. Pulling a chair over to the bed, Rachel sat. She reached through the side rails on the bed to hold Julie's hand. It felt cool to the touch.

"It's me, Rachel," she told her aunt. "I wanted to see how you're doing. Avery, the man I've been seeing for two years, just flew out to work on a case in Idaho. He's in the FBI, remember?"

Rachel shook her head at herself. Of course, Julie wouldn't remember. But she knew talking to her as if all was normal was good for her aunt.

"I'm doing fine, and my book cover design business is booming. I can't believe how busy I've been. And Jules is in her third year of college. Can you believe that? It's like just yesterday, she was a little girl. The time really does fly by."

Aunt Julie blinked at Jules' name, but she didn't move. Her eyes continued to stare at the ceiling.

"Well, I just wanted to see how you were doing and let you know that we're all fine. I miss you, Julie. And Jules does too. We love you." Rachel nearly choked up at the last words because it hurt so much to see Julie this way. She did truly love her aunt, but she wasn't here anymore. She was fading away.

Rachel heard the outer door open softly and then saw Shirley poke her head in.

"How's Miss Julie doing?" Shirley asked in her soft southern accent. She'd been Julie's main caretaker over the past two years, and Rachel had grown close to her.

"No response," Rachel said sadly.

Shirley nodded, and her brown curls bobbed as she did. "We can talk when you're done visiting," she told Rachel.

Rachel stood and moved the chair back. Then she patted her aunt's hand. "I'll be back to see you soon," she told Julie. "Jules and I love you." Brushing away tears, Rachel left the room and joined Shirley on the sofa.

"I'm sorry, dear," Shirley said. "Your aunt hasn't been doing well. We take her out on little walks in the wheelchair and try to get her to eat. But she doesn't respond. I'm afraid it's only a matter of time."

Rachel nodded as she wiped her tears with a tissue. "I understand, but it's still hard watching her fail so quickly. Just last year, she could still remember my name. Now, nothing."

"I know it's hard. This disease is terrible. But we are doing our best to ensure she doesn't suffer," Shirley said.

"Thank you," Rachel said. "I'll come by as often as possible. And will you call me immediately if she has a turn for the worst?"

"Of course I will," Shirley said. Both women stood and hugged. "It has been my honor to care for your aunt. She is very special to me."

"I couldn't have placed her in more loving and capable hands," Rachel said.

"Thank you, dear," Shirley said. "I'll be in touch."

Rachel drove away from the care center with a heavy heart. She wished there was more she could do for her aunt. As soon as she returned home, she'd call Jules and let her know how Julie was doing. Rachel knew Jules would want to visit her soon.

It was almost noon by the time Rachel returned home and pulled into her garage. She walked into the kitchen through the connecting door and placed her purse on the counter. Pulling out her phone, she remembered she'd shut it off last night and had forgotten to turn it back on.

The moment the phone came to life, it rang. Jules was calling.

"Hi, honey," Rachel said. "I was just going to call you."

"Mom?" Jules sounded anguished.

That one word sent chills up Rachel's back. "What is it? Are you okay?"

"I'm fine. I've been trying to call you. Mom, Amber never made it to her parents' house last night. They called me this morning and said she hadn't come home. She left at noon yesterday. It's only a four-hour drive." Jules sounded even more desperate as she spoke. "Mom. Amber is missing."

CHAPTER TWO

Rachel's heart pounded at the news Amber was missing. It was every parent's nightmare. Amber and Jules had been friends since junior high school, and she was like family.

"I'm so sorry, honey. You've spoken to Amber's parents?" Rachel asked.

"Yes. Several times. They're so worried. Atlanta police have put out a description of Amber and her car to local and state police, but that's about all. They did call the Tallahassee Police Department, and they are also on the lookout. Otherwise, it's just wait and see," Jules said, sounding frustrated. "Most of my friends are gone for break, and I didn't want to go out looking alone."

Rachel let out a sigh of relief. "That's smart of you. I'll come to your place as soon as possible, and we can drive around together to see if we can spot her car. While you're waiting for me, you could call the local hospitals to see if she's in one of those."

"Good idea," Jules said. "Mom? You don't think the killer has Amber, do you? I know the police responded quickly because of the local murders. I'm so scared for her."

Rachel was scared for Amber too. "Let's think positive until we have a reason not to," she told Jules, trying to sound as calm as possible. "She may have had an accident or even decided to visit a friend and forgot to tell her parents. There could be a hundred reasons why she's missing."

"She doesn't have friends between here and Atlanta," Jules said. "I know all her friends."

"Let's just think positive," Rachel said again, knowing how hard that would be. "I'll be there soon."

After she hung up, Rachel grabbed a jacket, purse, and some walking sneakers then jumped in the car and took off. She wished Avery was still there so she could bounce ideas off of him. As far as she knew, he was still in the air on the way to Idaho. Needing to talk to someone, she told her phone to call Lieutenant Jack Meyers, a friend who worked at the Panama City Beach Police Department. As soon as he answered, she felt relieved.

"Hi, Rachel. How are you doing?" Jack asked, sounding happy to hear from her.

"Hi, Jack. I'm fine, but someone I know isn't. My daughter's best friend, Amber, is missing. How much do you know about the murders happening around Tallahassee?"

Jack went right into detective mode. "All the police departments are keeping in touch about those murders. Quite honestly, they are more widespread than just Tallahassee. There are missing girls from Miami, Tampa, and even one from here. Tell me what you know."

Rachel told him the little she knew. "Any ideas on what we should do next?"

"It wouldn't hurt to drive the route you think she may have

driven and check gas stations for her car," Jack said. "Even though the police are on the lookout, they may miss it in plain sight. She may even have broken down in an area where her cell phone doesn't work. Do you have a picture of her? Send it to my cell phone, and I can send it out to patrol cars around here."

"I do. As soon as I get to Jules' apartment, I'll send it to you. Thanks for your help. I'll keep in touch," Rachel said.

"Any time. You know you can count on me," Jack said before they ended the call.

Rachel heard the warmth in his voice. She did know she could count on him. But she needed to keep it professional and not make it personal. She didn't like leading him on. They'd worked together last year on a case of a supposedly dead husband who was stalking his ex-wife, and they'd grown close. Even though Rachel had made it clear she was in a relationship with Avery, she knew that Jack still had feelings for her.

Rachel pulled up to the street where Jules' apartment complex was. She parked and buzzed the gate to be let in. Moments later, she was in Jules' apartment, hugging her daughter.

"Any word from anyone?" Rachel asked.

"No. And Amber isn't in any of the local hospitals," Jules said. Her long auburn hair was pulled up in a ponytail, and she was dressed simply in a long sweater, leggings, and sneakers. To Rachel, she looked young and afraid.

"Well, at least we know she's not hurt," Rachel said. "So we can go to the next step. Jack suggested we drive the route we think Amber would have taken out of town and stop at the gas stations to look for her car. Also, he said she may have broken down in an area with no cell reception. There are a lot of reasons she didn't make it home yet."

"I know," Jules said, looking suddenly exhausted. "I'm just so scared for her. Her father is driving down the highway out of Atlanta to see if he can spot her car."

"That's good," Rachel said. "Let's do the same driving out of Tallahassee. Hopefully, we'll find her unhurt."

They followed West Tennessee Street to highway 319, which took them north to highway 75, pulling into every gas station they saw and driving around them to look for Amber's car. At the fifth gas station, they stopped for a moment because Amber's mother had called Jules. Jules put it on speakerphone so Rachel could hear.

"Any luck yet?" Jules asked Camille Johnston. She held her breath, looking hopeful for good news.

"I'm afraid not," Camille said. "Ray drove a far way down 75 but with no luck."

Jules sighed. "I had hoped he'd find her. We're driving up that same route here, checking all the gas stations, and looking for her car. We haven't found it yet."

"That's good news, though, right?" Amber's mother sounded stressed. Who wouldn't be with their daughter missing? "The Tallahassee police think we should come there, but Atlanta P.D. thinks we should stay home. I'm at a loss as to what to do."

"Camille, this is Rachel." Rachel spoke up. "I'm so sorry this is happening, and we're doing everything we can think of to find her."

"Thank you," Camille said. "I'm just so scared. If someone took her," Camille's voice cracked. "I just don't know what we'd do."

Rachel's heart went out to her. She'd be a mess, too, if Jules was missing. "Why don't you wait one more night before coming down here?" Rachel suggested. "A lot can happen in twenty-four hours. Then you'll know if you should stay home or come here. It's hard, I know. But until the police find something, there's not much you can do here."

"That's true," Camille said. "I'll talk to Ray and see what he wants to do. Thank you both for looking for her. But please be safe."

"We will," Jules said. "And we'll keep in touch."

"Thank you, dear," Camille said before hanging up.

Jules looked over at her mother. "I don't know if I want to find her car unless she's in it." Tears filled her eyes.

"I know, dear. It seems like a lose-lose situation." Rachel wasn't sure if they were actually helping by looking for Amber's car, but there had to be something, somewhere, to show where the young woman was.

They continued driving and circled several more gas stations. It was late afternoon, and they knew they should turn back soon.

"Just one more," Rachel said, driving north on the highway. Up ahead was a clean-looking station that seemed like one a woman would feel safe stopping at. She pulled in and made her way around where the semi-trucks filled up, through a large lot where truck drivers could park and rest, then around to the other side of the building. As she passed a row of cars parked up against the gas station, Jules hollered, "Stop!"

Rachel stomped on the breaks. Parked between an old pickup truck and a large SUV sat a small, red car. Rachel stared at the make and model name on the trunk. Toyota Camry. "Does it look like Amber's car?"

Jules looked pale as she nodded. "That's her FSU sticker in the back window. Either that, or it's a coincidence."

Rachel took a deep breath and put the car in park. "I'll go look inside the car. You stay here, okay?"

Jules nodded. She looked frightened.

Stepping out of the car, Rachel checked the area to make sure no one was around. She didn't see anyone, so she walked up to the driver's side of the Camry. Inside was a woman's purse, a phone being charged, and the keys lying on the seat. Rachel's heart sank. She recognized the purse as one Amber had used often when the girls sometimes went out to dinner with Rachel.

Jules rolled down the window. "Mom?"

Rachel turned to her daughter as chills covered her entire body. "Call 911, honey. Tell them we've found Amber's car."

* * *

Two police officers arrived fifteen minutes later. One was a tall male officer, and the other was a female officer of average height, her dark hair in a bun underneath her uniform hat. Rachel had gone inside the gas station before they'd arrived and asked the cashier if she'd seen a young African American woman with long, spiral curls and brown eyes come inside. The woman shook her head no, but when Rachel mentioned the red Camry parked at the side of the building, the woman nodded. "That was there yesterday, too. We were supposed to call to get it towed today, but I've been too busy to do it yet."

Rachel told the police officers what she'd learned from the clerk.

"Did you touch the car?" the female patrol officer asked, frowning.

Rachel shook her head. "No. I didn't touch anything. I

only looked inside the window."

"Good." Her partner looked up the license plate number and nodded to the female officer. "It belongs to an Amber Johnston."

The officer, who introduced herself as Officer Patricia Wilson, gave Rachel the once over and then said, "Stick around a few minutes. I'd like to ask you a few questions."

Rachel nodded. "I'll be over by my car. Amber is my daughter's roommate, so she's pretty upset right now."

Officer Wilson glanced over at Jules. "I'm sorry. We won't keep you long."

Rachel went back to Jules and hugged her tight. "This still doesn't mean she's been hurt," she told her daughter. "We have to keep up hope."

Jules wiped her eyes. "It doesn't look good, Mom. It's hard for me not to think she's been kidnapped or worse."

"I know, dear. But I don't think we can process the worst right now. Let's just let the police do their job and see what happens."

"I should call Mrs. Johnston," Jules said. "She needs to know we found the car."

Rachel thought about that for a moment. If her daughter was missing, she'd rather hear it from a friend than from the police. "Let me call her. It's too painful for you right now."

Jules nodded.

Camille picked up her phone immediately. "Any news?"

Rachel took a breath to steady herself. This was the worst phone call a parent ever had to make or receive. "Hi, Camille. It's Rachel. We found Amber's car, but not her. I'm sorry. The police are looking at the car right now."

"Oh, my God!" Camille tried to stifle a sob. "Okay. I'll try to stay calm. Were her things in the car? Are you sure it's hers?"

"Yes, it's her car," Rachel said gently. "Her purse, keys, and phone were still in there."

"You don't think," Camille stopped speaking.

"I'm not going to think the worst until I'm told it," Rachel said. "I know that's a hard thing to do. My head would be swimming if it were Jules. Let's see if the police find any clues as to where she might be."

"We need to come down there," Camille said with certainty. "Whatever is going on, we need to be there to help."

"I think you should," Rachel told her. "And you're welcome to stay at my house or the girls' apartment."

"Thank you," Camille said. "I'll keep in touch. Please tell the police to call us the minute they learn anything."

"I will." Rachel said goodbye with a heavy heart. She couldn't imagine how difficult this was for the Johnstons. She hoped she'd never have to find out.

Officer Wilson came over and spoke with Rachel and Jules, asking why they searched for the car and how long they'd known Amber. They answered as best they could. Rachel finished by giving the officer Camille and Raymond's phone number so they could contact them when they learned something.

"We will," the officer said. "I just spoke to headquarters, and they'll be towing the car and going through it with a fine-tooth comb. We need to find this young woman fast. Call us if you hear anything." She gave them her card.

"We will," Rachel promised.

After Officer Wilson left, Jules turned to her mother. "Now what?"

"We're going back to your place to pack a bag so you can come home until this is solved," Rachel said. "No arguments."

Jules stared at her mother for a moment. "Okay. I think I'd feel safer at home."

Rachel was relieved. "Me, too. If someone took Amber—and that's a big if—then it means they were stalking her and knew where she lived. I don't want to lose you, too."

"I'm scared for her, Mom. What if," Jules paused.

"Come on. Let's get your stuff and not think about that, okay?"

They got in the car, and Rachel drove back to her daughter's apartment all the while praying that Amber would be found safe.

CHAPTER THREE

O nce Rachel and Jules arrived home, Rachel called Jack to tell him what she knew so far.

"I'm so sorry," Jack said, sounding upset. "What can I do to help?"

"I'm not sure at this point," Rachel told him. "I don't know if they'll decide to pursue this as her being taken or as a missing person's case. I'm at a loss as to what to do."

"Where's Avery? Has he spoken to the FBI task force about this yet?" Jack asked.

"I had just taken him to the airport to go to Idaho," Rachel said. "He's been assigned to the serial killer case there. He won't be able to help me here."

"Then let me see if I can come there for a few days and help," Jack said. "Even if it's just to help search for Amber."

"I can't ask you to do that," Rachel told him gently. "The police here are working on it."

"You didn't ask me, Rachel. I offered. Besides, we've had a similar missing woman's case around here. My boss might agree that it would be helpful for me to look into this one."

"Honestly, I'd feel better if you were here for a while," Rachel said. "You'd know the questions to ask that I wouldn't."

"I'll pack a bag and come," Jack said.

"Plan to stay at the house. Jules is here too," Rachel told him. "And Jack? Thank you."

"You know I'd do anything for you, Rachel," he said.

Rachel took a beat. It was getting too personal. "We're doing this for Amber," she said.

"Of course," Jack said, sounding all business again. "Can I bring Captain, too? He hates the kennel."

Rachel laughed. "I don't blame him. And I'll feel even safer with a German Shepherd in the house. Of course, you can bring him."

"See you soon," Jack said before hanging up.

"What did Jack think?" Jules asked. She'd met him last year while she was in Panama City Beach with her mother and had liked him.

"He's coming for a couple of days to see if he can be of any help. He can stay in the guest room," Rachel said. "He's bringing his dog, Captain, too."

This made Jules smile. "No one will mess with us with Captain around."

Rachel's phone buzzed, and she saw it was Officer Wilson. "Hello?" she answered anxiously. Rachel hoped they'd found Amber.

"This is Officer Wilson," the woman said. "I thought you might like to know that we're forming a search party tonight, and we need as many volunteers as possible. There's a big empty lot behind the gas station, and other searchers can go up and down the streets. Can you round up some helpers and come too?"

"Yes," Rachel said. "My daughter can ask her friends. Amber's parents won't be here for at least four hours; otherwise, I know they'd be first in line."

"Well, maybe it's better they aren't here, if you know what I mean. But I'm glad to hear they're coming to town," Officer Wilson said. "The FBI task force has also been notified, and the agent in charge is coming. If we don't find any clues tonight, they'll do another search tomorrow. Time is of the essence."

Rachel knew what they were thinking—if Amber had been abducted, they needed to find her fast. The thought gave her chills. "We'll be there as soon as we can."

Rachel turned to Jules. "We're going back to the gas station to help with the search. They're trying to be quick about this. Can you ask friends to come help?"

Jules nodded and immediately started texting everyone she knew who was still in town.

Rachel quickly changed into jeans, a warm sweater, and sensible sneakers and grabbed a jacket. She texted Jack telling him where they'd be if he showed up early. Then she and Jules hopped in the car and headed down her long driveway.

At the end of her driveway, which was on the dead end of the cul-de-sac, Rachel stopped when she saw a small black van slowly circle the road and then take off. As she waited, the driver stared directly at her. She frowned. It was the type of van that didn't have side or back windows. There was no business name painted on it. Rachel wondered who it was and what they were doing in her quiet neighborhood.

Her mind quickly returned to the task at hand, and she drove out to highway 12 and headed east to 319. It was late afternoon by the time they pulled into the gas station, where several patrol cars and other cars were now parked. Rachel grabbed two flashlights from her glove compartment and handed one to Jules. "In case it gets dark while we're searching," she told her.

Officer Wilson and her partner, Officer Jenkins, were standing by the squad cars talking with the other officers and the volunteers. Rachel approached the officers as Jules went to join her friends who'd shown up for the search.

"Glad to see you here," Officer Wilson said. "We managed to get a lot of people here quickly, which is good. We'll get started in a few minutes."

"My friend may show up later, too, with his German Shepherd," Rachel told her. "He's a homicide detective in Panama City Beach."

The officer smiled. "Great. The more, the merrier."

Rachel went over to Jules and was introduced to her friends. A few of them she'd met in passing while at Jules' apartment, but it was nice meeting the others. As she waited for the police to start the search, Rachel glanced around the area. The field behind the station was large, and the grass was waist high. It would be easy to hide someone in there. That thought didn't sit well with her. As she mulled that over, her phone buzzed. It was Avery.

"Hey, are you okay?" Avery asked, sounding worried. "I got to my hotel room and turned on the television, and there you were, standing with a group of people getting ready to search for Amber. How long has she been missing?"

"Television?" Rachel turned and glanced around, then saw the local television station's news van on the far side of the gas station. "Goodness. I had no idea they were here. They haven't approached anyone that I know of," she told Avery. Then she explained what she knew so far. "We're heading out to search the area with the police. I don't know if I want to find anything or not. Finding Amber in the tall grass would mean she was," Rachel broke off.

"I know," Avery said gently. "But maybe someone will find a clue. I'm glad they're working quickly on this. I just wish I could be there with you, helping. I'm sorry I'm not there."

"It would be nice if you were here, but you have your own work to do. I should tell you, though, that I called Jack for advice, and he's heading here for a couple of days. He and his dog will be staying in my guest room."

"Oh," Avery sounded surprised. "Well, it's a good idea for him to be there, despite my feelings about it. He can keep you and Jules safe. After all, if someone took Amber, he may have been stalking her, and they'd know Jules is her roommate. I hope she's staying at your house, too."

"She is. I'm not letting her out of my sight."

"Okay. Well, I'll let you get to it. Call me tonight if you get a chance, and let me know what's happening, okay?" Avery said.

"I will. I love you," Rachel told him.

"I love you, too. Don't go falling for that homicide detective, okay?"

Rachel laughed. It felt good to laugh after the day they'd had. "I won't." She said goodbye, and they hung up. She wished Avery was there, but there wasn't anything she could do about it.

A black SUV pulled in and parked beside the patrol cars. Stepping out of it was a man in a dark suit with a short haircut. He was of average height and slender, but he still looked imposing with his suit and sunglasses. It was obvious to Rachel he was FBI.

"Attention, everyone," Officer Wilson called out to get the

crowd's attention. "Gather around for instructions. We're ready to begin."

Rachel turned to Jules, who took a deep breath. Her daughter reached for her hand, something she hadn't done in years, and they walked together to where the officers were standing.

"Thank you all for coming," Officer Wilson said. "Special Agent Darren Carver from the FBI is here." He lifted his hand to the crowd as if no one would know the guy in the dark suit was FBI. "He's in charge of the task force that has been working to find the person or persons responsible for the recent murders of young women in the area. We're not speculating that Amber Johnston's case is classified as one of those cases, but it helps to have everyone involved. We'll pass out reflective vests to all of you and flashlights to those who didn't bring their own. Each officer here will take a group to a specific location to search. They'll explain what you need to do. So, let's get to work."

Rachel and Jules looked at each other, and Rachel could tell Jules was willing herself not to cry. She squeezed her daughter's hand. "We will find Amber," she told her.

Jules nodded.

Rachel and Jules were sent to the group that was going to walk the open field. Other volunteers would walk up and down the streets showing Amber's photo to the various businesses. The field group was led by Officer Jenkins, who told them to form two lines of ten people, each an arm's length apart. The first line would begin walking slowly, searching, and the second line would start several feet behind and search again.

Rachel took her job seriously, walking slowly and flashing her light in the grass. She hoped the light would catch something that she might not otherwise see. She noted that Jules was doing the same. It was slow going through the tall grass, but they took their time. People called out occasionally, but all they'd found was a water bottle or pop can. One man found a sock. The officer did bag each item to be checked later.

The sun was setting as the group in the field finished their search. Across the lot, Rachel noticed a smaller black SUV pull into the gas station. When the man got out, she instantly recognized the tall, muscular frame of Jack Meyers. Rachel waved at him, and he waved back, then let Captain out of the back of the vehicle and leashed him before heading across the field.

"That's my friend, Lieutenant Jack Meyers from the Panama City Beach Police Department," Rachel told Officer Jenkins.

"Great," the officer said. "Is that a search dog?"

"I don't think so, but maybe he can help," Rachel said.

"We'll take all the help we can get," Officer Jenkins said.

Rachel and Jules walked over and greeted Jack with hugs. "Thanks for coming," Rachel said. "We've already searched the field, but nothing substantial was found."

Officer Jenkins greeted Jack with a handshake. "Is your dog a trained search animal?"

"No, not officially," Jack said. "But I can walk him around the field and see if he senses anything."

"Okay. We'd appreciate it," Officer Jenkins said. "I'm sure the FBI will have search dogs out here and in other areas tomorrow, too."

As the group dispersed toward the parking lot, Jack began to walk Captain slowly up and down the field. Rachel and Jules headed back through the tall grass to the parking lot.

"Is that your friend?" Officer Wilson asked, nodding toward Jack.

"Yes. He's doing a sweep of the field with his dog," Rachel told her.

She nodded, then waved the FBI agent over. "Agent Darren Carver, I'd like you to meet Rachel and Jules Emery. Jules is Amber's roommate."

The agent shook their hands. His sunglasses were off, and he looked a bit more approachable. "It's nice to meet you two. Tomorrow I'd like to speak with you both about Amber Johnston. We're going to start searching again early in the morning, beginning right here if you want to join in."

"Sure," Rachel said. "We'll be here." Her phone buzzed, and she saw it was Camille. "It's Amber's mother," she told the agent before turning to take the call.

"We just got into town and are at the Hampton Inn on I-10. How is the search going?" Camille asked. Rachel had texted her about it before they'd headed out.

"We didn't find anything but the FBI will do another extensive search in the morning. I'm talking to the agent in charge right now. Is it okay if I give him your phone number?" Rachel asked.

"Yes, please. We want to be informed of what's going on as soon as possible," Camille said. "And thank you for inviting us to stay at your house. We thought it would be best to be centrally located here in town."

"I completely understand," Rachel said. "We'll talk soon." She hung up and turned back to Agent Carver, who'd been talking to Jules. "Let me give you Camille and Raymond Johnston's information. They'd appreciate it if you'd keep them updated."

"Are they in town now?" Agent Carver asked.

"Yes, at the Hampton Inn on I-10."

"I'll call them and drop by on my way back to my hotel," he said. He handed Rachel one of his cards to keep and one to write the Johnston's information on, then she handed it back.

From the edge of the field, Jack called Officer Jenkins over. Everyone watched as the officer hurried over and inspected something. Then he carefully bagged it.

"What was found?" Agent Carver asked as Officer Jenkins walked over to them. The officer handed the baggie to Carver. Inside was an amethyst bracelet with small, natural stones and a gold clasp. It was broken, but the stones had stayed in place.

Jules gasped. "That's Amber's favorite bracelet," she said. "She always wore it."

"Are you absolutely sure?" Agent Carver asked.

Jules nodded, struggling to hold back tears. "Yes. She bought it last year in Key West when we went there for spring break. It's definitely hers."

Rachel drew closer to Jules and rubbed her back. She knew this was a long, hard day for her.

Agent Carver studied the bracelet. "We know her car was here, so she must have struggled with whoever took her. Or she got away and is hiding somewhere, scared."

This made Rachel frown. "Why wouldn't she go for help or flag down a police car? If she did get away, wouldn't she have seen us searching and come out?"

Agent Carver turned his dark eyes on her, his mouth set in a thin line. "It was just an observation," he said. He pocketed the bracelet, turned, and headed for his car.

Jack was standing nearby with Captain on his leash. "Hm. The agent doesn't seem to like you," he said with humor in his voice.

"That's his problem," Rachel said. "What he said wasn't too bright."

Jack chuckled.

"Come on, honey." Rachel placed her arm around Jules. "Let's stop by your apartment and get the rest of what you'll need for the week."

Jules nodded.

"I'll follow you there," Jack said. "I don't want you going inside the apartment alone."

"Sounds good." Rachel got in her car with Jules, and they waited until Jack was in his car and ready to go. By now, most of the officers and searchers had left. The gas station looked deserted. Amber's car had been taken away, too, to be searched.

They drove the short distance to the girls' apartment, scanned Jules' ID to get through the gate, and pulled up into her parking space. Their place was on the second floor, so once Jack was out of his car with Captain, they headed up the stairs.

"Is there an elevator here?" Jack asked, glancing around.

"Yes. But most people use the stairs," Jules said. "It's quicker."

When they got to her door, Jules put her key in the lock. But when she turned the deadbolt, she looked up at her mother. "It's unlocked. I'm sure I locked the door when we left earlier."

"You did," Rachel said, her nerves tensing.

Jules pushed the door, and it swung open easily. The place was dark, and one look at the inner doorjamb told them everything they needed to know. "The door was forced open," Jules whispered. Someone had broken into the apartment.

CHAPTER FOUR

Jack went into police mode. "You two stay here. I'll go inside and check the place out."

Both women nodded and watched as Jack turned on his flashlight and led Captain inside. A few minutes later, he returned after turning on most of the lights. "Your place was ransacked," he said. "But there's no one here now."

Both Rachel and Jules walked into the entryway and gasped. The entire place had been torn apart. Furniture was overturned, drawers were opened, and everything else was lying on the floor.

"What on earth were they looking for?" Jules asked, looking stunned.

"I don't know," Jack said. "But it probably has to do with Amber's disappearance. You'd better report it to the police."

Rachel pulled out her phone and Officer Wilson's card. She answered in two rings. "Hi," Rachel said. "Are you still on duty?"

"I was just going to check out," Officer Wilson said. "Why?"

"Jules' apartment has been broken into and ransacked," Rachel told her.

"Text me the address, and I'll be there in a few minutes," the officer said.

Rachel hung up and texted her the address. "She's coming over in a few minutes," she told Jack and Jules. Rachel shook her head. "This doesn't make sense. If someone has Amber, then why did they need to tear up your place? What were they looking for?"

Jules dropped into a chair in the living room. She looked drained from all that had happened over the past two days. "I don't know. It's not like we have money or jewels stashed around here. We're college students. We don't have anything of value."

"This does seem strange," Jack said, walking around, being careful not to touch anything. "I hate to ask, but was Amber into anything illegal? Like drugs?"

Jules shook her head. "We don't do drugs, and Amber doesn't even drink. We never go out to clubs or bars. Mostly, we eat out with friends. Our friends are all serious students who are pretty boring."

Jack sat on the sofa across from Jules. "What about an ex-boyfriend? Is there anyone who would be angry at Amber?"

Jules frowned as she thought. "She dated a guy for a little over a year when we were freshmen, but after they broke it off, everything seemed okay. When we'd see him around, he'd wave and say hi. She's gone on dates here and there, but nothing serious. Amber takes college seriously and doesn't want anything to get in the way of her finishing. Boys are an afterthought right now."

Rachel was walking around the apartment looking for any clue as to what they were searching for while Jules and Jack talked. Clothes were strewn about, dresser drawers were dumped, and even their desks had been searched. But both girls' laptops were still there, along with their television and other electronic devices. The intruders weren't there to steal, that was for certain.

Officer Wilson arrived along with her partner, Officer Jenkins. "Goodness," she said, glancing around. "Someone did a number on this place. Is anything missing?"

"Nothing that I've noticed," Jules said. "I'll look around again to be sure."

"Their laptops and television weren't touched or anything else that could be pawned for money," Rachel said. "Unless Amber had some expensive jewelry."

Jules shook her head. "Amber didn't keep expensive jewelry here. She kept it at her parents' house. The pieces worth money had been handed down to her from her grandmother, so she didn't want to lose them."

Officer Wilson studied the broken doorjamb. "We might get some prints from this door handle," she said. "I'll call a team in to dust for fingerprints. It's a shot in the dark, but it's worth the trouble. I called Agent Carver to see if he wanted to come over here, but he was with Amber's parents, so he declined. But he found it interesting that you had a break-in."

They waited for a print expert to arrive, and Officer Wilson asked Jules the same questions Jack had. "It's so strange," the officer said. "If someone took Amber, why would they come to her place and ransack it? Although," she paused.

"What?" Rachel asked.

"Well, someone might have seen Jules at the search party on the news and took that chance to break in. It might not even be related to Amber's disappearance," Officer Wilson said. "But they were looking for something specific. Maybe money, jewelry, or drugs."

"Then they didn't find anything," Jules said, sounding irritated. "We have none of those things."

The officer nodded. "Did Amber have a passport?"

Rachel's brows lifted as she turned to her daughter. "You both have passports, don't you?"

Jules frowned. "Let me see if they're still here." She went into Amber's bedroom and checked through her dresser drawers that were spilled all over the floor. "It's not here," she called out to the others. Jules hurried into her own room and searched for her passport. She found it in her nightstand drawer, tucked into some other important papers. "They didn't take mine, though."

"It had to be the people who took Amber," Jack said. "But would they risk trying to get her on a plane with her passport? Her photo is all over the news right now."

"I'll report all of this to Agent Carver," Officer Wilson said. "His team has been studying the other cases, so he might have a better idea of what's happening."

Jules walked up to Officer Wilson. "So, you think Amber was taken by the guy or guys who took all those other girls?"

The officer placed a comforting hand on Jules' arm. "We don't know any of that for sure. But it's best if we treat it as such. The sooner we find your friend, the better."

Jules nodded and sat back down in the chair. Rachel's heart went out to her. She looked drained.

A few minutes later, the officer told them Jules could pack some of her personal items. "I took a few pictures," Officer Jenkins said. "We should be done here. But don't clean it up just yet in case another team will want to look around."

Officer Wilson said they'd also walk around the building

tomorrow and talk to the residents to see if anyone saw anything. "Are there cameras in the parking lot?" she asked.

"Yeah. A few. And one at the gate," Jules said.

"Good. We'll see if we can get footage from those, too."

Jules went to her room and packed clothes into a suitcase. She also packed what little jewelry she had, plus her laptop. She slipped her passport and other ID into her purse for safekeeping.

After the officers left, Jack studied the door. "Do you have a key for the lock on the door handle?" he asked Jules. "At least we can lock that. Tomorrow, I'll come over early and fix the doorjamb so I can put a new deadbolt on."

Jules nodded. As they left, she locked the door handle, and the three of them, plus Captain, walked down to their cars.

Rachel and Jules didn't speak much on the way home. Rachel knew her daughter was exhausted. When they walked into the house, Jules went straight to her room. Rachel followed.

"Do you want anything, hon?" she asked.

Jules shook her head. "I think I'll just go to bed. I want to be up early to search for Amber. And I also might go see the Johnstons if they aren't at the search."

"That's a good idea," Rachel said. She hugged her daughter. "We will find Amber."

"We don't know that, Mom," Jules said. "But I will hope for the best."

"Lock your window and pull the curtains," Rachel said. "I'm not taking any chances tonight."

Rachel closed her daughter's bedroom door and walked softly to the kitchen. Jack had brought in his duffle bag and was feeding Captain. "Want a beer?" she asked him.

"Absolutely," he said.

They each opened a bottle and went to sit in the living

room. Captain followed them after eating his food and laid down on the floor beside Jack.

"Thank you for being here," Rachel said. "I think I'd be scared out of my wits by now if it was just Jules and me here."

"I'm glad I came." Jack took another sip of his beer. "This is so much worse than I'd first thought. We've had young women disappear and end up at their boyfriend's house or somewhere else safe. But this is the real deal. I really believe that Amber was taken."

"It's so hard to grasp that," Rachel said sadly. "I've known Amber since she was in middle school. She's a sweet, intelligent young woman, and I don't want to think about some horrible person taking her. I can't imagine the nightmare her parents are living right now."

After they'd both finished their beers, Rachel showed Jack where his room was, and he picked up his duffle bag and called for Captain to follow him inside. "Thanks for putting me up here," he told Rachel. "Tomorrow's going to be another long day."

"You're welcome," Rachel said. "Try and get some sleep."

He gave her a sweet smile, then closed the door. Rachel headed to her own room. She was so exhausted. She changed and fell into bed. Setting her alarm for six a.m., Rachel fell into a deep sleep.

The next morning, they were all up early and had a quick breakfast. Rachel turned the television on to a news channel to see if anything more had been learned about Amber's case. While they ate, she turned up the volume when she saw Agent Carver standing behind a podium for a news conference.

"There's no word yet about the missing woman, Amber Johnston," he said into the microphones. "If anyone has seen or heard from her in the past two days, please contact us at the number on the screen. We are doing everything in our power to bring her home."

A few reporters asked him questions, most of which he evaded. Then he said, "Jonathan Danvers is with me today to make an announcement." Agent Carver moved aside and let the tall, handsome man take over the microphones.

"Who's he?" Jules asked.

"One of the richest men in the country," Jack said, sitting forward in his chair. "Why on earth is he there?"

"Hello, everyone," Danvers said, smiling wide. "As you know, I try to help as many people as possible since I'm fortunate to be able to afford to. I've been following this series of missing young women, and it's time this stops. I'm offering a one-million-dollar reward to anyone who can turn in information on either Ms. Johnston's case or any of the other cases so we can catch the culprit. Someone out there knows something. Please, call with whatever information you have. Thank you."

"Wow. That's a lot of money," Rachel said. She turned to Jack. "Do you think it'll help?"

He shrugged. "Rewards can somethings get people to speak up, but I think if someone knew something, they would have already called in a tip. As far as I'm concerned, this guy is just looking for more attention than he already gets."

Rachel's brows rose. "You don't like Jonathan Danvers much, do you?"

"I don't even know him," Jack said. "But there's just something about him that bothers me."

Rachel turned off the television. "Let's get ready to head out. Hopefully, today will have a happier ending."

Jack offered to drive them, so they got into his mid-sized SUV, and Captain sat in the back end. They went directly to the gas station again, where Officer Wilson had told them to go. Today, the area was packed full of police, volunteers, and even the FBI. Professional search dogs and their handlers were there, too.

"Sorry, boy," Jack said to Captain. "Looks like your services won't be needed anymore."

They were standing behind Jack's vehicle with the back open for Captain. Rachel petted the dog. "Don't worry. We can use you," she crooned.

Jack chuckled. "Don't baby my dog. He'll get used to it." This made Rachel smile.

Officer Wilson and Agent Carver stood in the back end of a pickup truck to get the crowd's attention. Officer Wilson spoke first. "Thank you to everyone who came. We really appreciate your help. Today, we're going to go over the same areas as well as a few others. I'll let Agent Carver explain."

"We've had dozens of tips so far this morning since Mr. Danvers offered his reward, and we thought we could split this group up to check out all the areas," Agent Carver said. "So, stay where you are, and we'll divide you into groups and give you your assignment." He hopped off the back of the truck and handed out maps to the other officers and agents. They went to work choosing their groups. Then, Agent Carver walked over to Rachel, Jules, and Jack.

"I'm glad to see you all here," he said, glancing over at Captain in the vehicle. "We have our own dogs here, but maybe we can put yours to use too."

Jack nodded.

"I didn't tell everyone this, but we've been keeping an eye

on the big and small airports around the area, and so far, no one with Amber's description has been seen getting on a flight or a private plane. With all the publicity happening for this case so quickly, I think it's safe to say they are still in the area or have driven out of the area. No airplanes."

"Why take her passport, then?" Rachel asked.

Agent Carver assessed her a moment before answering. "I suppose they thought they could go to an airport in another state and get her out. But since this has become a national news story, and they just stole the passport yesterday, then that plan may have changed."

Jack frowned as he thought. "Wait. I thought the suspect in the missing women cases was considered to be a serial killer. It would be just one person. Plus, if he was going to kill her, why wait two days, steal her passport, and try to get on a plane?" He directed his stare at Agent Carver. "Is there something you know that we don't?"

The agent's head snapped back as if he'd been physically slapped. "All of this is speculation. I said they, but I meant he. And quite frankly, we're still looking at all the possibilities."

"Then why are the girls found dead a few days later near where they were kidnapped?" Jules asked.

The agent looked flustered. "We've been putting in thousands of man-hours between the Florida State University Police, the Tallahassee Police Department, and our FBI agents for over eight months trying to solve these riddles. It's not all cut and dried. There are more questions than answers. So, let's just keep our focus on finding your friend, okay?"

Rachel glanced over at Jack, and he did the same to her. Something sounded off, and they both knew it. Before the agent could speak again, Camille and Raymond Johnston walked over to the group.

"Camille. I'm glad you're here," Rachel said, hugging Amber's mother. There were hugs all around, and Rachel introduced Jack to the couple. "Are you here to help with the search?" Rachel asked.

"I'd prefer if the parents didn't participate," Agent Carver said. "It would be better if they stay with me at ground zero."

"We want to help," Camille said sternly. "We can't sit around and do nothing."

"I agree," Ray said. "I'd feel better if I could help."

Rachel smiled over at Amber's parents. Camille, who worked as a paralegal in a prominent law firm in Atlanta, was a powerhouse when she had to be. She was tall, slender, and very pretty with her dark, smooth skin and expressive brown eyes. Ray was also tall but lanky and wore dark-rimmed glasses. He worked as an accountant in a small firm, and his pale skin proved it. But he was also a determined person. Together, they'd built a good life and gave their daughter a wonderful sense of self and standards to live her life by.

"Why don't you join our group?" Rachel suggested. "As soon as we get our orders from one of the officers."

"That would be wonderful. Thank you," Camille said, looking grateful to be included.

"Fine," Agent Carver said curtly. "But I still think the parents should stay with me." He walked away, looking like an angry child, and it was hard for Rachel not to laugh.

"Boy, that guy doesn't like us," Jack whispered to Rachel. "I guess we ask too many questions."

"The problem is, why isn't he asking those questions of his team?" Rachel said.

Officer Wilson came over and handed a map to Jack with

three places marked. "We've had a lot of tips, many about some old mom-and-pop motels on the fringes of town. Personally, I agree that's the type of place someone would hide out in because most will take cash and not ask questions. But wouldn't you think whoever took her would have gotten out of town by now?" she shook her head. "Anyway, if you could go to these three places and search, maybe ask questions if you see anyone, that would be great. Don't knock on doors, though." She looked at Jack. "I know you're a trained policeman, but I don't want anyone else in the group to get hurt."

"I understand," he said.

She nodded. "Call us if anything looks off. We'll send a patrol car."

They agreed. The Johnstons went to their car and followed Jack, Rachel, and Jules across town to the first motel.

For three hours, they searched around the old motels, asked the desk clerks questions, and then the maids if they saw one. All of the places looked deserted, with no cars in the parking lots. If anyone had stayed there the night before, they were long gone. Jack went across the street to a couple of diners to ask questions, but still no luck. At the third motel, after they'd finished, Rachel offered everyone a bottle of water from the cooler she'd brought.

"This is awful," Camille said, sounding defeated. "I want to find out where she is, but I'm afraid of what we might learn, too."

"I'm so sorry," Rachel said. "I can't imagine what you're going though. I know how upset I am over Amber's disappearance, but it would be multiplied by a thousand for you two."

"We're trying to keep our heads straight, though," Ray said. "We can't afford to fall to pieces right now. But it's hard."

Camille nodded and put her arm around her husband.

"Agent Carver was at your hotel last night. What did you think of him?" Rachel asked.

Camille raised a perfectly shaped brow. "Are you wondering if we think he's competent?"

"To be honest, yes," Rachel said.

"I thought he talked in circles," Ray said. "He's been heading this task force for months, and it sounds like they don't have a clue what's going on. I get that there hasn't been much evidence to follow. The girls are found without a mark on them and no fingerprints or DNA either. But there has to be something."

"I agree," Jack said. "Even a pattern to the kidnappings would help. I get the feeling he doesn't believe it's just one guy. And he's touchy if you ask him questions."

"What do we do, though?" Camille asked. "He's all we have."

"That's true," Rachel said. "But I'm still going to be on him until he starts coming up with answers. I can come up with a hundred questions for him."

Jack chuckled.

"Yep. That's my mom. She'll find Amber if the entire police force and FBI don't," Jules said, grinning.

"You won't have any complaints from me," Camille said. "I think I'll interrogate Agent Carver too. I'll put all my experience watching lawyers in the courtroom to work."

They all laughed about that.

It was late afternoon by the time they went their separate ways. Rachel called Officer Wilson to let her know they hadn't found anything. Then they drove back to her house, feeling downhearted to learn that no one had come up with any clues.

"Should we call for a pizza, and I'll make a salad?" Rachel asked as they entered the house.

"Yeah. That sounds good," Jules said. "I'm going to change into sweats." She headed for her room.

"Let me pay when it comes," Jack said, moving toward the kitchen to feed Captain. "You shouldn't have to feed me."

"I don't mind," Rachel said. "I'll be back in a minute." She walked toward her bedroom, but Captain began sniffing the air and pushed past her. "What's up with him?" Rachel asked Jack.

"Captain! Get back here, boy," Jack called. But the dog continued sniffing down the hallway toward Rachel's bedroom.

Jack rushed to grab him, but Rachel stopped him. "What if someone is in here?" she whispered. He nodded, and they both followed Captain into the bedroom. At the door of her walk-in closet, Captain stopped and barked.

Jack moved to the door, pulling his gun from its holster hidden under his overshirt. He signed for Captain to move away, and the dog obeyed. In one swift moment, Jack pulled open the door and pointed the gun inside the closet. "Who's in there?" he yelled.

From the fading light coming through the bedroom windows, Rachel saw a figure curled up in the back of her closet.

"Don't shoot," the female voice said.

Rachel knew that voice immediately. "Amber?"

The girl lifted her head and stared at Rachel. "Am I safe yet?" she asked in a small voice?

CHAPTER FIVE

Jack immediately holstered his gun, and Rachel ran into the closet and hugged Amber. "Oh, my goodness. We've been looking everywhere for you. Are you okay?" Rachel looked her over but couldn't see much in the darkened closet. She led her out to the bedroom and had her sit on the bed.

"What's going on in here?" Jules asked, then squealed when she saw Amber. "You're safe! I'm so happy to see you." She hugged her best friend, and Amber hung onto her as if for dear life.

Rachel could see now that Amber had been through a rough time. Her jeans and red shirt were ripped and dirty, and her usually curly hair was matted. "We should let you clean up and change clothes," Rachel said as Jules pulled away from hugging her friend. "Honey, would you have anything that Amber could wear?"

"Sure," Jules said. "Let me go get you something." She hurried to her bedroom.

Rachel and Jack eyed each other over Amber's head. Rachel sat on the bed beside her. "Are you okay?" she asked gently. "Did they hurt you?"

Tears filled Amber's eyes. "They drugged me, but they didn't touch me," she said softly. "They said they were saving me for someone else."

Rachel let out a sigh of relief. "So, they never managed to get you to where they were taking you?"

Amber shook her head. "From what I heard, too many people were looking for me, so they couldn't get me to an airport to fly me out. That was their words."

"Thank goodness," Rachel said.

Jules came in with clean clothes and a brush for Amber's curls. "Would you like to shower before you change?" she asked her friend.

Jack spoke up. "I hate to say it, but the police might want to see Amber before she changes. That way, if there's any evidence on her, they can collect it."

Amber turned and stared at Jack with wide eyes. "No. No police!" she shook her head vehemently.

Rachel instantly placed her arm around her. "Why, Amber? We have to tell them that you're safe so they'll stop searching."

Amber looked terrified. "No. We can't trust the police," she insisted. She looked up at Rachel with her deep brown eyes. "We can't trust them. They may be in on it."

Rachel, Jules, and Jack stared at her, stunned.

"Okay, honey," Rachel said. "We won't call anyone yet. Why don't you get cleaned up, and we'll place your clothes in a plastic bag in case the police need them for evidence. Then you can tell us what happened. Okay?"

Amber looked relieved and nodded.

"Is it okay if I call your parents to come over here? They've been worried sick," Rachel said. "We can all hear your story together."

Again, Amber nodded. Then she turned to Jules. "Will you stay in the bathroom with me while I shower? I don't want to be alone."

"Of course," Jules said.

"I'll leave Captain in here, too," Jack said. He pointed to his dog to sit by the bathroom door, and Captain obeyed.

Jack followed Rachel to the kitchen. "How are you going to get Amber's parents here without the police wondering what's going on?"

"I'll invite them over for dinner," Rachel said. "Hopefully, no police or FBI are with them right now." She hit Camille's name on her contacts, and she answered after a couple of rings.

"Hi, Camille," Rachel said, trying to sound normal. "Would you and Ray like to come to the house for dinner? We're ordering a pizza and have salad and thought you might want a break from everything."

"Oh, that's very nice of you," Camille said. "But I think we'll stay here in case there's any word."

"Please, Camille," Rachel said, her tone growing urgent. "I think you'll want to come here. It's important."

There was silence for a beat, and then Camille spoke. "Well, okay. We'll be there as soon as we can."

"Thanks. We'll see you in a few minutes." Rachel hung up and looked at Jack. "They're coming. Let's order pizza."

By the time the pizza had arrived, so had the Johnstons. Rachel spoke quietly with them for a few minutes, telling them what had happened. When Amber came out to the kitchen, her parents ran to her and hugged her, both crying.

"Thank the dear lord," Camille said, tears falling down her cheeks. "I thought we'd lost you."

"I thought I'd never see you again," Amber said, hugging

her parents.

Rachel had gone around the house and closed all the drapes and shades to ensure no one could look in and see what was happening. From this point on, she knew she couldn't trust anyone.

After a time, Camille said, "Shouldn't we call Agent Carver? He'll want to know Amber has been found."

"Not yet," Rachel said. "Let's all sit and try to eat something and let Amber tell her story." She turned to Amber. "If you're ready to."

Amber nodded. They all sat at the dining room table, but no one moved to eat. Amber stared at everyone, looking unsure as to where to start.

Rachel helped. "When did you get to the house today? And how did you get inside?"

"I finally found my way here sometime this afternoon. I remembered you had a key hidden under the flowerpot at the back door, so I used that to get inside," Amber said.

Jack stared over at Rachel, and she grimaced. "I know. It's not safe, but at least it helped Amber," she told him.

"I hid in the closet because I wasn't sure if the two men who took me were still searching for me. I didn't want anyone to see me here," Amber said, still looking fearful.

"That was smart," Rachel told her.

Camille placed a loving hand on Amber's arm. "Can you tell us everything that happened?"

Amber took a breath. "I had stopped at a gas station to fill up and get a snack. It looked like a safe place to stop. After filling up, I parked at the side of the building and went inside. When I came out, there wasn't anyone parked near me. I opened the door and tossed my purse inside, but someone grabbed me from behind before I could get in. I struggled a moment, enough to see one of the men's faces. But then the other man poked my arm with something, and I suddenly felt dizzy. The next thing I knew, I was slowly waking up in the back of a darkened vehicle with no windows."

Rachel was taking notes as Amber spoke. "You said you saw the guy. What did he look like?"

"The guy I saw was wearing a Florida State University Police uniform. I knew his face. I've seen him all over the campus. I never saw the other guy's face, but he had a regular Tallahassee Police uniform on. That's why I don't want to call the police. How will we know who else is in on it?" Amber asked.

Rachel looked over at Jack, who was frowning. She could practically read his mind. No one liked a dirty cop, especially another officer.

"Where did they take you?" Rachel asked, gently prodding Amber to continue.

She shook her head. "I'm not sure. We kept driving around, and I was out cold for half the time. From the little conversation I heard, they were supposed to take me to the Tallahassee airport and put me on a private plane. But they had to wait for the plane to arrive 'from the island'—their words—and that's what messed things up. By the time the plane arrived, everyone was already searching for me. They couldn't take the chance to go there."

"I'm surprised they let you hear all this," Jack said.

"It was open between the front seats and the back end," Amber said. "After the first time I began to stir, the University policeman told the other guy to give me more meds. He did. So, the next time I started to wake up, I was quiet and pretended I was asleep. That's when I heard them talking. I realized the only way I was getting out of there was to pretend to be drugged and then make my escape."

"Oh, my goodness," Camille said. "You must have been so scared."

"I was," Amber said. "And the university cop kept telling the other one to give me more meds, but he refused. He told him that too much in such a short time could kill me. The university cop laughed at that and said one way or another, I'd be dead soon anyway. That was all I needed to hear to know I had to make an escape. So, I kept pretending to be asleep, and they seemed to have forgotten about me."

"How did you escape?" Ray asked.

Amber took a sip of her soda and continued. "Yesterday, around dusk, we pulled over, and the university cop got out and walked away to make a phone call. The other cop opened the back doors to check on me. They hadn't tied me up because they figured the drugs were all they needed. He crawled into the back of the van to check my pulse, and that's when I took my chance. I pushed him hard and knocked his head into the side of the van. Then I slid out and ran. We were on a highway with woods on either side. I had no idea where I was, but I headed for the woods and ran as fast as possible. The cop I hit was overweight, so he couldn't run as fast, and the other one didn't see me go until I was already far away. I heard them yelling at each other, then trying to follow me, but I kept moving. I ran through the woods, following the highway until it got dark, then I hid in a copse of small pine trees. I couldn't hear them calling or running anymore, so I thought I was safe. I just had to get through the night and figure out where I was."

"That's amazing," Jules said. "You were so brave."

"I was scared to death," Amber said in a small voice. "But I had to try."

"I'm so proud of you," Rachel said. "To have the strength to escape like that while under such stress and drugged is amazing. How did you find my house?"

"I stayed there all night, and the next day, I took a chance and walked near the highway to see what road I was on. I realized I was near your neighborhood. Thank goodness I knew the area. So, I walked, being careful to stay hidden, and then got to your house in the afternoon. I was so relieved when I saw your house, I cried. I even fell asleep in the closet, waiting for you to come home."

"You're incredible," Camille said, hugging Amber. "I'm just so happy you're safe."

Her father hugged her too. Both parents looked so relieved.

Slowly, everyone began to dish up food and eat while Amber continued to answer questions.

"Can you tell us again what you heard the two men saying?" Jack asked. "Anything they said could be relevant." He'd already gotten a pad of paper and a pen from Rachel to take notes as she had.

"Like I said, they talked about how the plane was late to Tallahassee, and by the time it arrived, the news of my disappearance had already spread around. So, the university cop was on the phone constantly with someone, trying to figure out what to do," Amber said. "They talked about other airports where the private plane could land. That was why they'd headed north. I heard something about them going to Georgia to find an airport."

"And you said they mentioned an island?" Rachel asked.

Amber nodded. "They said they had to get me to the island

where the guy was waiting. But they never mentioned any names."

"You know for certain the man in the university police uniform is an actual police officer there?" Jack asked.

"Yes," Amber said with certainty. "He's always walking or driving around campus, talking with the female students. Some girls think he's just being nice, but I thought he was creepy." She turned to Jules. "You know the guy. Tall, skinny, pale. He has red-blond hair and skin with freckles. He's losing his hair, so he has a combover."

"Him? Oh, my goodness." Jules said, looking shocked. "We all thought he was a creep, but he was the one who abducted you?"

"It was definitely him," Amber said. "I saw him straight on, and he was angry about that. I didn't see the other guy's face. But he was shorter, maybe 5' 8" tall and heavyset."

"Hm." Jack looked thoughtful. "It sounds like he knew something about sedatives, too."

"Maybe he was pretending to be a policeman," Rachel said. "He could have been a paramedic or trained as a nurse."

Jack nodded his agreement.

"We need to tell the police this, so they'll pick up that university policeman," Camille said. "He's a danger to other young women."

"And he's probably still looking for Amber," Rachel said. "He knows the minute she talks to anyone, he'll be caught."

Amber looked frightened. "But what if he's not the only police officer involved? What if you report it, and someone else comes after me?"

"We'll keep you safe, dear," Ray said.

"These guys have guns. Someone is paying them to abduct

women. They might come here and kill us all," Amber said, growing agitated.

"They might do that anyway," Jack said calmly. "We have to report this and then get you to a safe place."

"What about Agent Carver?" Camille asked. "He's the head of the task force trying to solve these cases. And he's not associated with the local police."

"He's working with the local and university police, though," Rachel said. "I'm not saying we shouldn't report it, but we must be cautious of anyone we talk to."

Everyone nodded.

"I think Camille is right," Jack finally said. "Let's ask Agent Carver to come here and talk to Amber with all of us here to protect her. Then he can do what he needs to do. But I think afterward, we need to find a safe place for Amber to hide."

They all agreed, so Camille made the call.

CHAPTER SIX

Agent Darren Carver arrived at Rachel's house forty-five minutes later. He hadn't been told why he was asked to come, so when Rachel opened the door, she could see he was annoyed.

"What is so important I had to trudge all the way up here so late at night?" he asked as he entered.

"Follow me," Rachel said, leading him into the living room. When Agent Carver saw Amber, his eyes grew wide.

"Is this Amber?" he asked, staring first at Rachel, then at Camille.

"Yes," Rachel answered. "And she has a very interesting story to tell."

Agent Carver pulled his phone out of his pocket. "I must alert the police to stop the search." Rachel quickly placed her hand over his phone.

"Whatever you do, don't tell anyone where she is. You'll understand after she's explained," Rachel said.

His eyes narrowed at her.

"It's for her safety," Rachel said.

He gave a curt nod and then made the call. After Agent Carver hung up, he pulled a pad of paper and a pen from his pocket and found a place to sit. "In all honesty, I'd rather do this at the station," he said.

Amber's eyes grew fearful.

"No," Rachel said. "Listen to her first."

"Fine. Go ahead. Where have you been all this time?" the agent asked.

Amber slowly began telling her story again. Agent Carver didn't ask many questions, only nodded and grunted as she spoke. He asked her to clarify a couple of things she'd heard the men say, but that was about it. After she finished, he asked her to describe the university policeman.

Amber gave him the description as the agent wrote it down. Everyone in the room waited for Agent Carver to react in some way.

"And you're sure you heard correctly that they were trying to fly you out of here on a private plane?" Agent Carver asked, his eyes boring into Amber's.

"Yes," she said. "That's why they still had me in the van. Because they couldn't get me out of here."

"Hm." He set his notepad down on his lap. "Why would they want to fly you out of here if they're the serial killers? All the other girls were found two to five days later, close to where they'd been abducted. Why would they take you in a plane to kill you and then bring you back?"

Rachel looked over at Jack and saw his contempt for the agent on his face.

"Did it ever occur to you that they're trafficking these girls somewhere, then bringing them back to kill them?" Jack asked, staring hard at Agent Carver. "It wouldn't be hard if they're using private planes."

Agent Carver grunted. "Who in their right mind would pay that much money to traffic one girl somewhere, then send her back to kill her? What would be the gain there? Traffickers want to make as much money as they can off each girl. One gig? That sounds ridiculous."

"Not for a very rich person, it doesn't," Rachel said. She was getting more annoyed by the minute.

Agent Carver turned to her. "It isn't logical. Amber's story doesn't fit the profile of what we've been investigating. This may have been a botched abduction, and the guys got scared. I don't think it has anything to do with our serial killer."

Jack snorted. "Yeah. Your task force has been successful so far in finding the killer, right?"

Agent Carver ignored him and stood. "We'll pick up the university policeman and talk to him. That's the most we can do." He turned to Amber. "Until then, I want you to stay in the area so I can speak with you again." He pocketed his notepad and headed for the door.

Rachel was stunned by his attitude. She stood and followed him. "You're not even going to consider anything else other than a serial killer? You have a young lady here who's been abducted, and you're just going to ignore it?"

"I'm not ignoring it. I said we'd pick up the guy. But what evidence is there to prove he actually did this?" Agent Carver asked.

Rachel thought about Amber's clothing and the bracelet they'd found during the search. The guy's prints could be on those things. But she didn't want to give anything to Agent Carver. She didn't trust him. When she didn't reply, the agent went out the door to his car.

"Can you believe that guy?" Rachel said as she rejoined the group. "He's not even listening."

"He seems to have his mind set on one thing only and won't consider any other possibilities," Camille said, looking frustrated. "It appears obvious to me that something other than a single serial killer is what's happening."

"Me, too," Jack said. "Amber said the university policeman had said she'd be dead eventually. That means they're taking young women somewhere and then killing them and dropping the bodies near where they'd been abducted."

"It does sound like a lot of work just to bring a girl somewhere for a day or two," Rachel said. "But it wouldn't be unheard of. Jeffery Epstein flew girls all over to use them. The only difference is he didn't kill them."

They all went silent, thinking about that.

"Now what?" Jules asked. "If Agent Carver doesn't take this seriously, those two kidnappers are still looking for Amber. What do we do tonight?"

"I think we should all stay here tonight. Safety in numbers," Rachel said, glancing over at the Johnstons. "Would you be okay with that?"

Camille looked over at her husband for a moment, then nodded. "Yes. If you don't mind."

"Not at all," Rachel said. "I'll bunk with Jules and set up my room for the three of you. I'm sure you'll feel safer with your daughter near you."

Camille nodded. "Then what?"

Rachel stood. "I'll make some coffee, and we'll discuss a plan. If we all agree that the girls need to go somewhere safe, then let's figure out where."

Jules looked up. "Girls? Me too?"

Rachel nodded. "You and Amber live together. It wouldn't be too far-fetched to think you might be on their list, too. Besides, wherever we figure out to hide Amber, she'll need a friend."

Jules nodded. "Yeah. We should stick together." She glanced over at Amber and smiled.

Rachel headed to the kitchen to start a pot of coffee and then to her room to change the sheets on her bed. Camille joined her and helped.

"Do you really think it's necessary to hide the girls somewhere?" Camille asked. "We could take Amber home. She'd be safe there."

"Those kidnappers know where you live. They may be desperate. And if Agent Carver doesn't pick up the university police officer immediately, he'd be free to hunt Amber down. I think hiding them is the only safe answer."

"Where?" Camille asked.

Jack came into the room. "I think I know the perfect place."

Both women looked at him, and Rachel smiled. This was a team effort, and she thought they were lucky to have Jack on their side.

* * *

That night after everyone had settled into bed, Avery called Rachel. She slipped out of the bed she was sharing with Jules and went into the bathroom.

"Hi," she said, relieved to hear from him. Rachel knew he couldn't help, but it was nice hearing his voice.

"Hi." His voice was warm and caring. "Have you heard anything about Amber?"

Rachel filled him in on everything that had happened that day, and Avery was relieved Amber was safe. "What's so strange was Agent Carver's reaction. It's as if he didn't want to tie Amber's abduction in with the other murders. Amber is a witness to who abducted her, and the agent couldn't care less."

"Agent Carver," Avery said softly. "Is that Darren Carver?"

"Yes," Rachel said. "Do you know him?"

"His name is familiar, but I can't quite figure out why. Let me do some checking, and I'll let you know. Until then, I'd try to keep him away if your instincts are telling you something is wrong."

"I agree. He didn't even ask for any evidence. We bagged up Amber's clothing in case there was evidence on it to tie the two policemen and the van to her abduction. I'm not sure what to do with it now."

"Is there a police officer you trust? I'd give it to him or her. If the FBI isn't interested, the police could follow up with their own investigation," Avery said.

"Good idea. I was thinking about the officer who led the search for Amber. She seemed on the up and up. It's terrible when we can't trust any of the area police," Rachel said.

"There're bad eggs in every organization," he said. "Is Jack still there?"

Rachel laughed softly. "Yes, he is. And so are the Johnstons, Amber, Jules, and of course, Captain. We're all having a sleepover."

"Good to hear," Avery said, chuckling. "Safety in numbers. I'll call you tomorrow if I find out anything about Carver. Keep safe, okay? No playing at being a detective and getting yourself hurt."

"Hey, I don't play at being a detective—I'm actually very

good at it," she said, teasing him. "But yeah, we're all going to play it safe until that policeman, and hopefully the other guy, are captured."

"Good. I miss you," Avery said. "I hate being this far away."

"I miss you, too. I'd feel better if you were here," Rachel said. "But you have a job to do."

"Yeah. And as much as I hate to admit it, I'm glad you have Jack there."

"He's been a lot of help," she said. "Don't worry—I may fall in love with Captain, but I'll still love you, too," she teased.

After they said goodbye, Rachel felt better than she had all day. She was almost certain their plan would work, and they could keep Amber safe. Almost.

* * *

The next morning, the group put their plan into action. The Johnstons went back to their hotel room to pack and check out and then stopped again at Rachel's house before leaving for Atlanta. Jules and Jack left to buy a new deadbolt for the girls' apartment, and Jules packed clothes for herself and Amber while he replaced it. Rachel, Amber, and Captain stayed at the house with all the doors locked and the outside security cameras on. Rachel was happy to have Captain for added security.

Soon, everyone returned to the house.

"I hope we're doing the right thing," Camille said, glancing over at her husband for support. "I'd feel better if Amber was with us."

"I'd never want you to do something you don't feel comfortable with," Rachel said. "If you aren't sure, we can do what feels right to you."

"Mom," Amber spoke up, her voice stronger than it had been since she'd returned. "I think Jack and Rachel are right. If I go home with you, something could happen. Hiding out somewhere that isn't connected to you, dad, or Rachel is the best way. No one would even think to look for us there."

"My mother's house in Panama City Beach is the perfect spot for the girls," Jack said. "It's just two blocks from the beach, and it's on a quiet little cul-de-sac. She's away on a cruise with friends and won't mind us using it. Since it's not tied to either girl, it's the safest spot for them."

"Who'll be there to watch out for them?" Ray asked.

"There are cameras outside the house that I have access to on my phone. You can download the app, and I'll give you the password if that will ease your mind," Jack told Ray. "And I have a couple of trustworthy friends on the force who I can ask to drive by there often. They'll think I'm checking up on my mom, so they won't have to know the girls are there."

"Mom," Amber said. "I agree with Jack. This is our safest option. Once they catch those guys, I can return to my normal life."

Camille nodded. "Okay. I only want you to be safe."

"I know." Amber hugged her mother.

"We'd all better get moving before it gets too late," Jack said. He turned to Rachel. "Are you sure you're going to be okay alone here?"

"I'll be fine. In fact, I'm going to go visit Officer Wilson after you all leave. Then I'll be back here, locked in nice and tight."

"I'll be back tomorrow once I get the girls settled in," Jack said. "Captain can be your company."

Rachel smiled. "I like his company."

Everyone said their goodbyes with hugs all around. Rachel was going to miss Jules, but she knew this was the right thing to do.

Rachel pulled her car out of the garage, and the Johnstons moved theirs inside. In case anyone was watching the house, they didn't want them to see what was going on, or it would ruin their plan. They had taken an old life-size Barbie of Jules' and found a costume wig that would pass for Amber's curls. They set the Barbie up in the backseat on pillows for height and hoped it would fool anyone who might be watching.

"I knew that big Barbie would come in handy someday," Jules said, laughing.

After another long goodbye, Camille and Ray pulled out of the garage and drove away. Through the tinted windows, they couldn't tell if it was Amber or a decoy.

"Okay. On to the second part of the plan," Rachel said. Jack backed his SUV into the garage, and they loaded it with the girls' luggage. Both girls got into the back seat and laid down with a blanket over them.

"Keep them safe, okay?" Rachel said before Jack got in behind the wheel.

"I will. You be safe, too. Take care of Captain for me."

She smiled. "I will." They hugged, which was unusual for them but, at this point, seemed natural. Then, Jack drove away. Rachel closed the garage door and locked the house up until she was ready to leave. She prayed their plan would work.

CHAPTER SEVEN

Once inside the house, Rachel petted Captain's head. "Well, it's just you and me, boy," she said. Then she got her wallet out and found the card Officer Wilson had given her. She dialed the number, and the officer answered on the second ring.

"Officer Wilson," was all she said.

"Hello," Rachel said. "This is Rachel Emery. The mother of Amber Johnston's roommate. Would it be possible to meet up with you for a few minutes to talk?"

There was a pause on the other end. "Yes. We can meet somewhere. May I ask what this is about?"

"I'd rather not speak on the phone," Rachel said. "Where would be the most convenient place for us to meet?"

"There's a coffee shop on Monroe near the police station. I could meet you there in half an hour," she said.

"Great. I'll be there," Rachel said. After hanging up, she grabbed the bagged clothing she had from Amber and headed out the door.

It took Rachel almost the entire thirty minutes to reach

the coffee shop because of the traffic. When she entered, Officer Wilson was already sitting at a table near the back. Rachel walked there and sat across from her.

"Thank you for meeting with me," Rachel said. "You were the only person we could think of who we trusted."

Office Wilson looked confused. "I heard Amber was found. I'm happy she's okay. But we haven't been given any details yet from Agent Carver."

"That doesn't surprise me," Rachel said, trying not to sound angry. "He practically wrote off the entire episode saying it had nothing to do with the serial killer they're tracking. I'm not even sure if he's arrested one of the men involved."

Officer Wilson placed her elbows on the table, moving closer toward Rachel. "What man?"

Rachel shook her head. "See what I mean? Amber recognized one of the men who'd abducted her. He's a university police officer. She described him to Agent Carver, and we expected he'd arrest him, yet we haven't heard a word."

"We weren't told to be on the lookout for anyone," Officer Wilson said. "And we'd be the ones to look for this policeman, not Agent Carver."

"That's what I figured," Rachel said. "And he didn't ask us if we had any evidence." Rachel pulled the bag of clothing out of the shopping bag she'd carried it in. "These are the clothes Amber wore when they abducted her. If anything, there might be fingerprints or carpet fibers on them from the van."

The officer's brows shot up. "Van? Honestly, I've heard nothing about this. Is there a chance I could speak with Amber and get her report?"

Rachel shook her head. "She went home with her parents today. Amber doesn't want to talk to anyone. Frankly, she's scared of the entire police force. The other man who abducted her was wearing a Tallahassee police uniform."

"I see," Officer Wilson said. She pulled a notepad and pen from her pocket. "Please, tell me what you know, and I'll make sure we pick up this guy."

Rachel described everything to Officer Wilson as best she could. She also mentioned the bracelet that was found in the field behind the gas station. "Officer Jenson placed it in a small plastic bag, and I saw Agent Carver slip it into his pocket. There definitely has to be fingerprints on it since it broke off as Amber struggled with the men."

Officer Wilson frowned. "Agent Carver should have given that to us. Believe me, I'll make sure to get it from him and have all this evidence processed. He might be running the task force, but it's up to us to process evidence and make arrests."

"I'm relieved I told you," Rachel said. "We need to get that officer off the streets as soon as possible. And the other guy, too. What if they grab another girl?"

"I agree." Officer Wilson stood and shook Rachel's hand. "Thank you for trusting me with this information. I'll get on it right away."

"Thank you," Rachel said. The two women walked out of the coffee shop together, then said goodbye. Rachel got in her car and headed home.

Rachel drove up to her house and pulled into the garage. Captain greeted her at the garage door that entered the kitchen. "Hey, boy," she said, scratching behind his ears. "Any excitement while I was gone?" She walked to the hall closet to put her jacket away and stopped dead in her tracks. The front door had been jimmied open and was standing slightly ajar.

Rachel's heart pounded in her chest. Someone had broken

in. Were they still there? When something cold touched her hand, she jumped. Turning, she saw Captain standing there, smiling up at her. Rachel laughed. "Of course, no one got inside," she said to the dog. "I'll bet you scared the crap out of them."

Rachel pushed the door shut and locked it. At least the lock wasn't broken. Then she sat at the kitchen table with her phone and looked at footage from her outdoor camera. The first video showed nothing, but the second one did—a tall man with a combover was working on getting inside the house. Far behind him was a shorter, stockier man, but he'd kept his head down. Rachel could hear Captain barking in the video. Why had this man continued to try to break in? Didn't he believe the dog was real?

Another clip showed the bigger man yelling at the tall one that there was a camera. He looked up, and the camera got a perfect picture of his face.

"Gotcha," Rachel said, smiling. That's when the two men turned and ran down the driveway.

Now Rachel had the perfect photo to show the police. She texted the man's picture to Jack. *"Are you still with our friends?"* she wrote, not wanting to mention the girls' names.

Jack texted back. *"Just bringing groceries. Did that guy break in?"*

"No. The cameras scared him off. Will you see if he's the one?" Rachel texted.

"Will do. Stay safe!"

Rachel stood and walked around the house to make sure all the doors and windows were locked. She found a broom handle and placed it on the runner of the sliding glass door for added security. These guys weren't giving up their search for Amber, so she needed to take every precaution.

She sat down at her kitchen counter and texted Camille to tell her someone had tried to break in. *"Be extra careful. I'm sure they know where you live, too."*

Camille texted back, thanking her for the information, and said they would be careful.

"I'm glad I have you here," Rachel told Captain.

Rachel made herself a sandwich for lunch and sat down to eat it. Jack texted her as soon as she sat.

"That's the guy. Our friend confirmed it."

"Good. I'll contact Officer Wilson immediately," Rachel texted back. Then she called Officer Wilson for the second time that day.

"Officer Wilson," she answered.

"Hi. This is Rachel Emery again," Rachel said.

"Oh. What can I do for you?"

"My door was jimmied opened when I got home after seeing you," Rachel said. "And I got a video of the guy on my security camera. Amber confirmed he's one of the guys who abducted her."

"Really? Are you safe?" the officer asked.

"I am. Luckily, I have my friend's dog with me. I'm sure he scared them off, as well as realizing they were on camera. But we have a positive ID on the guy now."

"Can you text me the photo and video?" Officer Wilson asked.

"Yes, I can," Rachel said.

"Also, I talked to Agent Carver this morning. He hasn't done anything about the information you gave him yesterday. He also said he had no knowledge of a bracelet having been found. But when I talked to my partner, Jenkins, he said he remembered giving it to the agent, and he pocketed it like you said. So, I spoke with my superior, and she said I can take over the case with the evidence I have," Officer Wilson said. "With his photo, I will definitely be able to arrest him."

"That's good to hear," Rachel said. "I'll send it out right away. Will you let me know once he's arrested? I think we'll all sleep easier knowing he's off the streets."

"Yes, I will. I'll talk to you later," the officer said.

After they'd hung up, Rachel texted both the still photo and the video of the guy breaking into her house. She couldn't wait to hear that he was behind bars.

After eating, Rachel took Captain outside into the backyard to do his business and threw the ball for him a few times, then they went back inside to her office. Rachel had a few projects due soon, so she thought she could catch up on her work since she'd be home alone overnight. Normally, she worked at least five days a week on her book cover projects, but this week had been too upsetting for her to even think about work.

Captain fell asleep near her desk as she worked. Rachel felt much safer with the dog here. It made her wonder if she should get a dog of her own since she was usually home alone much of the time.

Rachel had been engrossed in her work for almost an hour when her phone buzzed. She smiled when she saw it was Avery.

"Hey there," she said. "It's good to hear from you."

"That's encouraging," he said. "Is everything okay there?"

"It is. I gave Officer Wilson the clothes Amber wore the day she was abducted so they could be checked for evidence. She was surprised that Agent Carver hadn't asked for them or told anyone to be on the lookout for the university officer. She's now taking charge of the case."

"Well, that doesn't surprise me," Avery said. "I'm glad they're looking for the guy now."

"And don't get upset, but that same guy tried to break into my house while I was with Officer Wilson. He didn't get in because he realized he was on camera, and it scared him off. I think Captain had a hand in scaring him away too. But I did get some good video and a still shot of him that I gave to Officer Wilson."

"Of course I'm going to get upset," Avery said. "But I'm glad he didn't get in. I suppose they were still looking for Amber. Hopefully, now the police will pick him up."

"That's what I'm hoping," Rachel said. "I'll feel better when they do."

"Me, too," Avery said. "I learned a little about Agent Carver."

This piqued Rachel's interest. "What?"

"He's not exactly the cleanest FBI agent in the country. About ten years ago, he was suspended for suspicion of collaborating with drug dealers. He was on the task force to shut them down, but his superior thought he was colluding with them instead. After a full investigation, they had no proof to fire him, so he was moved to homicide. His last big case was on a task force for a suspected serial killer in Los Angeles six years ago. But they never solved the case."

"Wow," Rachel said. "How does this guy keep his job? Now he's heading this task force and hasn't a clue who the killer is."

"I'll admit it's not always easy to wrap up a serial killer case, but I just have a bad feeling about Agent Carver," Avery said. "I'd say to stay away from him if you can."

"I agree," Rachel said.

They talked a little longer about his case and other things.

After Rachel hung up, she quickly searched for a serial killer in Los Angeles six years ago. The articles she found told of several young college women being murdered over a period of three years, and then it just stopped. The task force had to abandon the project because they never found a suspect they could pin it on.

Rachel studied the photos of the women who'd been murdered. The cases seemed similar to the ones in Florida—the girls vanished into thin air somewhere near their college and, several days later, were found dead close to where they'd disappeared. Unlike the Florida women, these ones were found with fingerprints and DNA evidence on them. Unfortunately, there were no matches found from the evidence.

The fact that the killings seemed similar bothered Rachel.

Jack called later that night to say all was well. He didn't mention the girls' names, and Rachel understood why—he didn't trust the phones weren't being tapped.

"I'm going to spend half a day at the office tomorrow and then head back to your place," Jack said. "I don't like thinking of you being alone."

Rachel laughed. "I'm not alone. I have a big, handsome boy here to protect me."

"I hope you're talking about Captain," Jack teased.

She laughed again. "Now that I know everyone is safe, I'm catching up on some work and hope to get a good night's sleep. I'll call you if I hear they've found the university policeman. Officer Wilson said she'd let me know."

"Okay. That sounds good," Jack said. "I was thinking, when I get back, we should look deeper into the murders. Compare the girls and their backgrounds and such. There has to be a reason each girl was chosen—like Amber. I don't believe it was just random."

"I agree. I've already been doing some research. We can share information tomorrow."

She said goodnight to him and went to make dinner. After feeding Captain, Rachel heated up a frozen dinner and sat at the counter, watching the television. The twenty-four-hour news cycle sometimes got desperate for news and was replaying the search for Amber. They reported she'd been found and was in a safe place. They replayed a quick interview with Agent Carver, in which he basically said nothing at all, and then a new spot with billionaire Jonathan Danvers. He repeated his offer of a one-million-dollar reward to anyone with information that would bring the serial killer to justice.

Rachel watched him, wondering why he was involved in the case. He was a tall, good-looking man in his fifties with silver hair and in good shape. She'd heard his name occasionally on the news for scholarships he'd sponsored and other money he'd given for disaster relief in both the Bahamas and Florida after hurricanes. Rachel didn't know why, but he seemed a little too slick for her. Or maybe she was just suspicious of everyone.

"He's probably the nicest man alive," Rachel told Captain. The dog gave her a cynical look, which made her laugh. "Or maybe not."

She finally went to bed, hoping everything would be solved soon and they could all return to their regular lives.

The next morning, Rachel switched on the television while she made coffee and fed Captain. As she sipped her coffee, a story caught her eye. She looked up at the television to see a picture of the exact man who'd been at her front door yesterday. Rachel quickly raised the volume.

"University Police Officer Carl Krigbaum was found dead

today at the side of the highway with one gunshot wound to the head. The Tallahassee Police Department hasn't reported much yet, but there is buzz that it may have been a suicide," the reporter on TV said. "More will be known after the official autopsy."

Rachel stared at the scene on the television, completely stunned. Their main suspect was dead.

CHAPTER EIGHT

Rachel called Jack as soon as she was over the shock of seeing their main suspect for abducting Amber was dead. "Did you see the news today?"

"I just did," Jack said. "It's hard to believe Krigbaum killed himself, solving the case so easily."

"I don't know if I should be relieved or scared to death of whoever killed him," Rachel said. "That person could now be after the people who identified him."

"Sit tight, and don't open your door to anyone," Jack said. "I'm going to report to my superior and then head out of here. Suspects don't just turn up dead. More than likely, he was a pawn in a game of murder."

"I'll be here," Rachel said. After hanging up, she went around the house again, making sure everything was locked. She didn't want to take chances with her safety. After showering, dressing, and letting Captain out in the backyard for his own morning routine, Rachel headed to her office to do more research.

She searched for information about the Los Angeles murders again and this time, printed out reports on each victim along with their photo. Looking at them, she was surprised at how different each woman looked. They were of different ethnicities, varying hair and eye colors, and even different heights and weights. That seemed strange to Rachel. Didn't serial killers tend to pick girls who were similar in appearance?

As her printer buzzed, Rachel read as many articles as she could find on the investigation. Halfway through a batch of articles, her eyes widened as she recognized another name attached to the Los Angeles case. It read, "Billionaire Jonathan Danvers, a resident of Malibu, CA, has generously offered a reward of $500,000 to anyone who gives information to the FBI that will lead to the arrest of the serial killer, also known as the 'Angel Killer.'"

"Both Agent Carver and Jonathan Danvers were involved in the LA serial killer investigation," Rachel said softly to herself. "Seems a little too convenient to me."

Captain had been sleeping next to the desk. He lifted his head and stared at her.

"Seems fishy to you, too, doesn't it?" Rachel asked the dog.

Rachel printed out that information to show Jack. Then she set her research to the more recent murders in Florida. She printed out the descriptions of all the murdered women.

--Jenelle Parkerson—Twenty-two-year-old blonde, blue-eyed senior from Tallahassee attending FSU.

--Chloe Drywer—Twenty-year-old woman with auburn hair and green eyes from Miami attending FSU.

--Kaelynn Jeffries—Nineteen-year-old tall, slender woman with dark black hair and brown eyes attending FSU.

--Jennifer Collins—Eighteen-year-old non-college student who lived near FSU. Short-haired blonde with green eyes and a curvy figure. Worked at a store near the college, and her roommate was an FSU student.

--Melanie Lopez—Twenty-one-year-old woman with long dark hair and brown eyes from Texas attending FSU.

There were a couple of young women missing in Miami as well, and one missing from Panama City Beach, but they weren't listed as the serial killer's victims. They had the same type of abduction and murder as the other women, though.

Rachel thought of Amber. An African American girl, average height and curvy, with a beautiful face, spiral curls, and brown eyes. Even though Agent Carver didn't believe she was on the serial killer's list—as far as Rachel was concerned, she was. Thankfully, she'd survived.

As Rachel stared at the list of girls from both Los Angeles and Florida, the only similarity she found between them was the fact that each was beautiful and uniquely different. Was the killer collecting beautiful girls who looked different? Or was there a serial killer after all? Maybe someone liked to collect girls, period.

"I can't wait to run this all by Jack," she said.

When Rachel's phone buzzed, she was so deep in thought that she barely even noticed it. But when she looked at it, her heart leapt. It was from the Magnolia Memory Care Center. Quickly, she answered it.

"Hi, Rachel?" the woman on the phone asked. "This is Shirley from the care center."

"Yes. Hi, Shirley. Is everything all right?" Rachel asked.

"I'm sorry, dear," Shirley said gently. "But your Aunt Julie isn't doing very well. The doctor came by and said it was only a matter of hours before we lose her."

Rachel took in a sharp breath. She knew this day was coming, but she still wasn't prepared. "I'll be there right away," she said.

"I'll be waiting for you, dear," Shirley said before hanging up.

Rachel glanced at the clock. It was a little after noon. Quickly, she changed clothes and let Captain out to do his business. Then she texted Jack to tell him where she'd be.

"I'm sorry," Jack texted back. *"I'll bring my stuff to your house and take care of Captain, then meet you there."*

"You don't have to come," Rachel texted.

"No. I don't have to, but I want to. See you there," Jack texted back.

As Rachel grabbed her purse, she wished Jules was still in Tallahassee so she could come with her. Rachel knew her daughter would want to be with her aunt at this time, but she didn't want to risk her or Amber's safety. After locking up, she drove south to the care center.

When Rachel arrived, Shirley met her at the door. The kindly woman hugged her close.

"I'm so sorry," Shirley said. "But I'm glad you can be here with your aunt. She may not know you're here, but it's still a comfort."

"Thank you, Shirley," Rachel said. "You've always been so good to Julie and me."

Shirley gave her a small smile. "It's my job, but I love each of the patients I care for."

Shirley escorted Rachel to Julie's room, then asked if she could get her anything.

"No, thank you," Rachel said. "A man will be coming by later, asking for Julie's room. If you could let the front desk know he's coming, that would be a great help. His name is Jack."

"I'll do that." Shirley left quietly down the hallway.

Rachel set her purse down and went to her aunt's—mom's—bedroom. Julie's frail body barely showed underneath the blankets. Over the months, she'd lost so much weight there wasn't much left of her.

"Hi, Aunt Julie," Rachel said softly, using the name Julie would recognize best. "I'm here." She pulled a chair near the bed and sat. Reaching for Julie's frail hand, she held it gently.

Rachel became lost in her childhood memories and how wonderful Aunt Julie and Uncle Gordy had been to her. She reminisced to Julie about all the good times they'd shared and how much she'd appreciated their kindness and love, especially after having lived with little affection at her first home. "I hope I've said I love you enough," Rachel told her as tears filled her eyes. "I hope you've felt loved and cared for these past few years."

Rachel didn't know how long she'd sat there when she heard Jack's footsteps cross the living room to the bedroom. He looked into the bedroom and whispered, "Are you okay?"

Those simple words brought more tears to Rachel's eyes. Jack kneeled beside her and wrapped his arm around her as her head fell on his shoulder. All the emotions of the day came to the surface the moment she saw him.

"I wish Jules could be here," Rachel whispered, brushing away tears. "Julie loved her so much."

"I'm sorry she can't be," Jack said. He moved a chair next to Rachel's and sat. "But at least we know she's safe, and that's what's important."

Rachel nodded.

Jack reached for her hand. "I'll stay with you."

Rachel should have told him to leave, but this was too much for her to deal with alone. Everything that had happened this week with Amber's abduction had drained her. And now she was losing Julie. She really didn't want to be alone. "Thank you."

They sat together next to Julie into the wee hours of the night. Shirley checked in on them and even brought them coffee and dinner. Rachel tried to eat a little, but she didn't have much of an appetite. She consoled herself with the fact that her aunt would not die alone. She was there with her, and she hoped her aunt could feel the love coming from her.

At one-fifteen in the morning, Julie's ragged breathing ceased. Rachel had fallen asleep on Jack's shoulder, and the sudden silence had woken her up. Jack pressed the button for the nurse, and Shirley came in. She'd stayed late past her shift to be there for Rachel and Julie.

She listened to Julie's heartbeat, then tried her pulse. "I'm sorry," Shirley said. "She's gone."

Rachel nodded, too exhausted to speak. She'd cried all evening and now had no tears left. Rachel stood and hugged Shirley, thanking her for caring for her aunt.

"It was my pleasure," Shirley said. "She was a wonderful person. I'm happy to have had the chance to know her." She smiled at Rachel. "Go home, dear. You can make arrangements for Julie's funeral tomorrow. Now, it's you who needs to rest."

Rachel nodded again, and Jack led her through the care center and to his car.

"We'll get your car tomorrow," he said. Rachel had no strength to disagree. She was thankful for Jack's presence.

Once home, Jack took care of everything. He fed Captain and let him out in the backyard. Then he pulled back the covers on Rachel's bed and told her to get a good night's sleep. "We can call Jules tomorrow. Tonight, you need your rest."

Rachel agreed. To Jack's surprise, she wrapped her arms around him and held him close. "Thank you for being with me tonight. I needed someone there with me."

Jack kissed the top of her head. "I was happy to do it," he said. "Goodnight."

They separated, and Jack left so Rachel could go to bed. She changed, then crawled under the covers, knowing she needed her strength for the next few days.

* * *

Rachel awoke to the smell of freshly brewed coffee. It took her a moment to remember she was home in bed, and when she looked at the clock, she was surprised she'd slept until nine.

Rising, Rachel put on a sweatshirt and sweatpants then padded down the hall to the kitchen. There stood Jack, freshly showered, and holding a steaming mug of coffee.

"Well, good morning," he said, offering her the mug. "You're lucky. I haven't touched this one yet, so it's yours."

"Thank you." She accepted the mug. Captain followed her to the counter, where she sat down. She rubbed his head and scratched behind his ears. "I could get used to having Captain around. He's quite the charmer."

Jack smiled. "What about me? Am I not as charming as a dog?"

She laughed. "Well, you can make coffee, and Captain can't, so I guess you win."

Jack came over with his own mug of coffee and sat next to her. "How are you feeling today?"

Rachel sighed. "Tired. A little lost. But I'm also glad that Julie isn't suffering anymore. I'll miss her, though. Even though she didn't know Jules or me over the past year, I'm still happy I could visit with her. It will seem strange not seeing her anymore."

"Loss is hard no matter how it happens," Jack said.

Rachel nodded. "I'll need to make some arrangements. And I have to contact Jules, too. I also did some research yesterday that I want to share with you."

"First things first," Jack said. He went to his room and came back with a plain-looking phone. "I gave both girls a burner phone with minutes on it so they wouldn't use their own, and I have one for you and me, too, just to be safe. You can call Jules on this."

"What a great idea," Rachel said, brightening. "Thank you."

Jack smiled. "Well, I do have some experience in investigative work."

This made Rachel laugh. "Yes. I'd say you have a little. But thank you for thinking of this. Even though the main suspect is dead, I still don't think Amber is safe. That other guy is still out there. And I found some interesting stuff, too."

"Can't wait to read it all. But family comes first," Jack said.

Rachel called Jules with the sad news of Julie's passing. Jules was upset and sorry she couldn't have been there for Julie and her mother.

"I know you would have wanted to be there, but it couldn't be helped," Rachel said. "At least she isn't suffering any longer."

"I know," Jules said. "But I'll still miss her."

"Me, too," Rachel told her. "I'll make her funeral plans for next week. Hopefully, it will be safe for you to come back by then."

"School starts up on Monday," Jules said. "We'll have to be back by then."

Rachel sighed. "Then I hope they find that other abductor by then. Otherwise, we'll all be on pins and needles."

Rachel reminded Jules to call her on the burner phone if she needed something. Then the two hung up. She turned to Jack. "I'll give you the articles I printed out, and you can read them while I shower."

"Great."

She handed them to him. "I think you'll find them interesting," Rachel said. Then she went to her room to shower and change. By the time she was done, Jack had read all the articles and had a few ideas of his own.

"But you'd better take care of your aunt's business before we dig into all this," Jack said. "I'll drive you to the care center to get your car."

Once there, Rachel went inside and settled a few matters with the care center, then asked them to suggest a funeral home. They did, and when she got outside to her car, Jack was still sitting in his SUV.

"You don't have to wait for me," she told him.

"If you don't mind, I'll tag along with you," Jack said. "Ever since your house was broken into, I don't trust anyone."

She nodded and got inside her car. He followed her to the funeral home and went inside with her while she made arrangements for Julie's cremation and a small, graveside funeral. They already had a plot purchased next to Julie's husband, Gordon.

Rachel set the date out a week for the funeral, hoping that by then, Jules could attend.

Once they left the funeral home, Rachel stood by her car, feeling lost. Jack seemed to understand.

"Let's get lunch, and we can talk about this case," he suggested. Rachel nodded and followed his car to a restaurant north of downtown Tallahassee. They went inside and found a booth in the back corner where they could talk privately.

After ordering their drinks and food, Jack pulled the papers out of a folder he'd brought along and set them on the table. "Are you sure you want to go through these now?"

"Yes," Rachel said. "Anything to get my mind off of Julie."

"Okay. I read all of these, and of course, the first thing that stood out was the fact that Agent Carver worked on the case in California but never found the serial killer. And that Jonathan Danvers offered a reward then, too," Jack said. "So, these two guys knew each other all those years ago. Seems fishy, doesn't it?"

"It does," Rachel said. "Avery thought it was odd about Carver being on that task force too. But he did say that it wasn't unusual for a task force to disband if they haven't been successful. There are a lot of suspected serial killers out there who've never been caught."

"I can understand that," Jack said. "But don't you find it odd that the California case and this one in Florida are so similar? Although, the killer or killers weren't as smart back then. Makes me wonder if we'd find the same fingerprints or DNA on those womens' clothing that might be found on Amber's."

"The dead officer—Krigbaum—worked as an LAPD officer during that same time, too," Rachel said. "He might actually be the fall guy for someone else."

"Hm," Jack looked thoughtful. "You know what else I

noticed? In both cases, the women disappeared on a Thursday or Friday, then their bodies were found early the next week, like a Tuesday or Wednesday. Every woman had been left somewhere easy to find—as if the killer wanted them found. Why would someone do that? Most serial killers hide their victims."

"Interesting," Rachel said. She glanced at the dates of the murders. "And they weren't killed right away. Their deaths were generally only 24-48 hours before they were found. That means they were alive over the weekend." She looked at Jack. "Why? So the killer could spend time with them before he killed them? That's unusual for a serial killer too."

Their food came, and they both ate as they continued to discuss the case.

"I think your theory that these murders have more to do with trafficking than with a serial killer is correct," Jack said. "Someone grabs a young woman, gets paid to bring her to someone else, then maybe takes her back after the weekend and kills her. Maybe there's big money in finding someone a weekend girl."

"And it seems as if these women are chosen on purpose," Rachel said. "Each one is beautiful, and each one looks completely different. Almost like someone requested a certain type of woman, and that's what they're brought." She sat silent a moment. "But this has to be someone with a lot of money. Grabbing a young woman and getting her on a private plane isn't cheap. Do you really think rich men would pay for such a thing?"

Jack shrugged. "Some men think they can buy anything. It wouldn't surprise me if someone rich was behind this."

"Someone like Jonathan Danvers?" Rachel asked. Their eyes met.

"We're going to have to find some solid proof before we even say that out loud," Jack said. "But yeah, a guy like that could afford it."

"So why put up the reward money?" Rachel asked.

"To cover his tracks," Jack said.

Rachel looked up, and her brows rose. "Speak of the devil," she said. "Danvers and Carver just came in here together."

"You're kidding." Jack turned to look, and there, sure enough, were the two men sitting in a booth on the opposite side of the restaurant. "What do you think they're up to?"

"I don't know," Rachel said. "But after we eat, we should find out."

CHAPTER NINE

Rachel and Jack finished eating and paid their bill. They walked across the restaurant and stood next to Agent Carver and Jonathan Danvers' table.

"Well, hello," Rachel said, noting the startled look on Agent Carver's face. "I didn't know you two were such good friends."

Agent Carver frowned. "Were you following me?"

Jack snorted. "Why would we follow you? We came here for lunch and saw you two come inside. Maybe you were following us."

Danvers stood and offered his hand to Rachel. "I haven't had the pleasure," he said smoothly. "I'm Jonathan Danvers."

"Rachel Emery," she said, shaking his hand. "And I know who you are. You offered a reward to anyone who could give information on the killers of the young women here in Florida."

"Ah. Rachel Emery. Your name is familiar," Danvers said, glancing at Carver.

"Amber Johnston is roommates with Ms. Emery's daughter," Carver said.

"Ah, I see. Well, I'm happy that Amber is safe. At least one person had a happy ending," Danvers said, smiling.

"I'm Lieutenant Jack Meyers," Jack spoke up, shoving his hand at Danvers. "Of the Panama City Beach Police Department."

Danvers shook his hand. "Well, it's very nice to meet you, Lieutenant. I see Ms. Emery is in very good hands." He smiled again. "Would you two like to join us?"

Rachel glanced at Agent Carver and saw a look of annoyance cross his face. "We'd love to, but just for a moment," she said, sliding into the booth next to Danvers.

Jack grabbed a chair and sat at the end of the table, blocking any chance for Agent Carver to escape.

Danvers spoke first. "I was catching up with Agent Carver on whether they've had any leads in the serial killer case. I don't just lend my money to help; I like to stay involved."

"Really?" Rachel asked. "Was it like that six years ago in California when you offered half a million dollars for leads for that serial killer too?"

"Yes," Jack said, staring at Agent Carver. "You were on that task force, too, weren't you?"

"Hm," Agent Carver grunted. "So, you've done your homework. It's no secret that I worked on that case."

"No, it isn't," Rachel said. "Unfortunately, that killer was never found. It's also no secret that the officer found dead yesterday morning, Krigbaum, was also working in Los Angeles with the LAPD. That's an awful lot of coincidences, don't you think?"

Agent Carver narrowed his eyes. "People move around all the time. Have you always lived in Florida?" he asked her pointedly.

"It's funny," Rachel continued, ignoring his question. "Neither you nor Officer Wilson contacted me about

Krigbaum's death. Considering I gave her information about his attempted break-in at my house, I'd think someone would have informed me of his death."

Carver frowned. "Break-in? I hadn't been told about that."

"I gave the information to Officer Wilson because she seemed more interested in the facts of this case than you did," Rachel said. "I gave her Amber's clothing as well. It might have evidence on it from the abductors."

"Well, you've been a very busy woman," Agent Carver said. "I was going to call you, though. I need to get in touch with Amber to identify Krigbaum as the man who'd abducted her. She's not answering her phone."

"I'll tell her you want to speak to her," Rachel said. "We aren't disclosing her location right now. Especially since you didn't seem interested in her case as part of your investigation. She doesn't feel safe."

"By the way," Jack said, staring at Carver. "Has it occurred to you how similar the California and Florida cases are? You should really look at your old files and compare the two cases. You'd be surprised."

Before Agent Carver could respond, Rachel turned to Danvers. "Do you still have a house in California? I'm assuming a man of your wealth would have houses all over the world."

Danvers chuckled. "Well, I do have a few, but I sold the Malibu home a few years ago when I bought the island in the Caribbean. I find it's far more beautiful than the Pacific Ocean, don't you think?"

"I wouldn't know," Rachel said. "I've never been to the Caribbean. I'm sure it's lovely."

Jack stood. "Well, we've taken up enough of your time. Enjoy your visit."

Rachel stood too. "Yes. It was nice meeting you, Mr. Danvers."

"A pleasure," he said smoothly. "But please, call me Jonathan."

Rachel nodded, smiled, then turned to walk away with Jack.

"Don't forget to tell Ms. Johnston to call me," Agent Carver called out at their retreating figures.

Rachel waved but kept on walking. Once they were outside, Rachel felt like she was going to burst.

"Let's wait until we get back to your house to talk," Jack suggested. "We have a lot to discuss."

Rachel nodded and got into her car.

As soon as Rachel was in her driveway, her phone lit up. Camille was calling her, and Amber had left a message from the burner phone. She went inside before returning any calls.

"What's up?" Jack asked after letting Captain outside.

"Camille called. And so did Amber. I'll call Camille if you'll use the burner phone to call Amber, okay?"

Jack nodded and went to get his burner.

"Hi, Camille?" Rachel said. "Is everything okay?"

"We had a break-in," Camille said, sounding shaken. "Ray and I left the house to get groceries, and someone got inside. They didn't take anything but made a mess. Thank God Amber wasn't here."

"That's awful," Rachel said. "I'm so sorry. But it doesn't surprise me. The university officer that was found dead tried to break into my house the other day. I have it on my security camera. I'll bet someone broke into your house looking for Amber."

"Well, now they know she's not here unless they think she was with us. I'm just glad she's safe," Camille said.

"Don't call her on your phones, okay?" Rachel said. "We can't trust anyone right now. Jack got us burner phones, so they can't be traced. Amber can call you on her burner phone too."

"She called us on it and explained not to call her. I'm glad you're taking every precaution. Who do you think broke into our house?" Camille asked.

"It has to be the other guy who abducted Amber. Maybe he doesn't know if she saw his face or not," Rachel said. "Until he's caught, she's still not safe."

"I got a call from Agent Carver this morning looking for Amber. I was vague about where she was," Camille said. "I don't feel like I can trust him."

"Me, too," Rachel said. "We saw him earlier today, and he asked about Amber. I didn't tell him how to find her. Did you get any security footage on the break-in?"

"No, unfortunately. The internet wires for the entire neighborhood had been cut this morning. Now, I know why."

"We'll keep you posted on what we find out," Rachel told her. "Until then, at least we know the girls are safe." The two women said goodbye and hung up.

"What did Amber call about?" Rachel asked Jack.

"She'd spoken with her mother and was worried about their break-in. I calmed her down," Jack said. "No one could even guess where the girls are, so I know they're safe."

Rachel nodded. "This is such a mess. Who do we trust?"

"No one," Jack said, looking grim.

Rachel turned on the news and left the volume on low. She wanted to see if there was any more information about the university police officer's death. "Don't you think that would be big news?" she asked Jack. "Finding an officer dead on the side of the highway usually is."

"It should be," he agreed. "But not if there's something fishy about his death. They'll keep that close to the vest, then. I'm interested in who is actually investigating his death—the Tallahassee police or the FBI."

"Agent Carver doesn't seem interested in investigating anything other than what he finds interesting," Rachel said with disgust. "He blew off Amber's abduction like it didn't even matter. I guess she would have been more interesting if she'd been found dead." Rachel shivered. Just the thought of Amber being murdered made her cringe.

"Luckily, she got away. Otherwise, I think it would have ended badly," Jack said gently.

Rachel nodded. All this talk about death was getting to be too much.

Jack grabbed the file of papers they'd been discussing earlier at lunch and opened it up on the coffee table. "So, how do we prove that Jonathan Danvers has something to do with these killings?" he asked. "Or if Agent Carver does."

Rachel went to make them each a cup of coffee, and they sat and re-examined the murders of each woman, both from California and Florida.

"Danvers said he had a place in Malibu back then," Rachel said. "I wonder how far it is from the UCLA campus where the girls were abducted?"

Jack got out his phone and studied the map. "Not as far as you'd think. By car, about fifty minutes."

Their eyes met. "And now he has his own island in the Caribbean. And possibly a private plane," Rachel said. "Could he really be trafficking young women?" It seemed hard to believe yet seemingly normal people had been caught doing such things.

A knock sounded on Rachel's front door, causing them both to jump. Captain stood up at attention. Rachel looked at the security app on her phone. "It's Agent Carver."

Jack quickly gathered their papers and placed them back in the folder while Rachel answered the door.

"Agent," Rachel said. "This is a surprise."

"May I come in?" Agent Carver asked, glancing around her to where Jack sat. "I need to talk to you both."

"Of course," Rachel moved aside and let him in. "Would you like some coffee?"

"No, no thanks." He seemed distracted as he looked around. "That dog won't bite, will it?"

Jack chuckled. "Only if I tell him to."

That didn't seem to calm Agent Carver's nerves.

"Don't worry, he's fine." Jack gestured to Captain to lie down, and the dog did. "What can we do for you, Agent?"

Agent Carver cleared his throat as he sat on the sofa across from Jack and Rachel. "I wanted to talk to you about today. I want to make it perfectly clear that I'm not friends with Jonathan Danvers. He continued to call me until I met up with him. He had a million questions about the murders and if we'd learned anything new. He was also interested in Amber Johnston's case."

Rachel's brows rose. "Is it normal for you to share information with outsiders?"

Agent Carver snorted. "No, it's not normal, but here I am, sharing with you two. Danvers thinks that because he offers a big reward for information, he has the right to be a part of the investigation. I'd prefer to keep him out of it."

"That's interesting," Jack said. "Was he like this during the investigation in California, too?"

"I wasn't the lead on that one, so I didn't talk to him, but he did keep coming to headquarters and bothering my superior." Carver ran his hand over his short hair. "These rich guys are just bored and want to be included. Basically, Danvers is a nice guy, just nosey."

"So, why are you telling us this?" Rachel asked.

"I didn't want you two to get the wrong idea. I'm not collaborating with the guy in any way. I was just trying to get him off my back."

"Excuse me for saying so, Agent," Rachel said. "But you seem like the kind of guy who doesn't care what other people think. Why care what we think?"

Agent Carver nodded. "Generally, I don't care. I do my job. But this afternoon, when you brought up the California murders and how they're similar to the ones here, that got to me. Believe me, I've thought the same thing. But I don't have the files from the California case to compare to the ones here. I thought you might share with me what you've learned."

Jack and Rachel looked at each other for a moment, then Jack shrugged. "All the information you need is on the internet. Rachel found information on both cases, and we've been comparing them." He opened the file folder and spread out the sheets. "We noticed a few similarities."

"Will you show me?" Agent Carver asked.

"Sure," Rachel said.

Rachel and Jack showed him the similarities they'd found between the murders. "And despite what you want to believe," Rachel said. "We still think this is more about trafficking young women than there being a serial killer. The murders don't follow the profile of a serial killer."

"You're an expert on serial killers?" Agent Carver asked snidely.

"No," Jack said sharply. "But there's no evidence this is a serial killer. These girls disappear for a few days and then are planted near where they'd been abducted, as if the killer wanted them found. It's not the same M.O. as a serial killer."

Agent Carver sat silent a moment as if considering this. "It could be that Carl Krigbaum was a serial killer along with his accomplice. As you said, he lived in LA during the other murders."

"Could be, except when they abducted Amber, they weren't interested in killing her immediately. They were trying to get her on a private plane. Their plan didn't work out, though," Rachel said.

"So, who owns the plane they wanted to get her on?" Carver asked.

"We don't know," Jack said. "We haven't gotten that far. And since it's officially your case, I'd think you'd want to find out what private planes came in and out of Tallahassee Airport around the time Amber was abducted. It might be interesting whose name you find."

Agent Carver stood. "I'll look into it. For now, though, we are working on who Krigbaum was and how he was connected." He narrowed his eyes at Rachel and Jack. "Contrary to what you believe, I am working to solve these cases. But I'm not going to jump to conclusions and ruin all the work the task force has done so far."

He walked toward the door, one eye on Captain to make sure the dog didn't follow him. "Thank you for sharing your information with me. I will take it into consideration."

Rachel nodded. She still didn't believe he cared one iota about what they'd told him.

"And I need to talk to Amber Johnston," Agent Carver

said. "Is she at her parents' house in Atlanta?"

Rachel thought a moment. "Did you hear that someone broke into their place?"

His brows rose. "No. I hadn't heard that. Why?"

"We figure they were looking for Amber," Jack said. "Luckily, she wasn't home."

"You think Krigbaum's associate was looking for her?" Carver asked.

"We don't know," Rachel said. "But it's a good guess. As long as that man is free, she isn't safe."

"We can offer her protection," Agent Carver said.

"She doesn't trust anyone right now," Rachel told him. "Not police or FBI. I can't blame her. She's safe right now, so we aren't telling anyone where she is."

"Hm. Okay," Agent Carver said. "You also said you'd turned in Amber's clothing to Officer Wilson. We'll need that to see if there is any DNA or fingerprints from Krigbaum on it."

"She has it," Rachel said. "And you have the bracelet."

Carver frowned. "Bracelet?"

"Yes. The one Captain and I found in the field by Amber's car," Jack said. "You put it in your pocket that night. If the abductors touched it, there should be a fingerprint on it."

"Ah, yes. Okay. I remember. We'll have it checked out too."

Agent Carver opened the door to leave, then turned around. "And I'd appreciate it if you both would back away from this case. It's not your case to solve. Let the experts work on it." With that, he headed for his car.

Rachel turned to Jack. "Should I send Captain out after him?"

He chuckled. "Better not, but I'd like to. What a jerk."

As she shut the door, her phone buzzed. "It's Officer Wilson," she told Jack.

"Hm. The plot thickens," he said with a smile.

CHAPTER TEN

"Hello, Rachel?" Officer Wilson asked.

"Yes, this is she," Rachel responded. "It's good to hear from you."

"I'm sorry I didn't get back to you sooner," the officer said. "I'm sure you've already seen that Officer Carl Krigbaum was found dead. I should have contacted you immediately, but things have been busy here."

"I understand," Rachel said. She wished she could put Officer Wilson on speakerphone so Jack could hear, but she didn't want to scare her off. "Has anything new been learned about him?"

"I'm sorry, but I don't have any information about him or his death. They are still trying to determine if it was murder or suicide. But I'm no longer on the case, so I haven't been in the loop," Officer Wilson said. "But I wanted to make sure you knew that he is no longer a threat to you or Amber Johnston."

"Thank you," Rachel said. "It's a relief that man won't be abducting young women anymore. I just hope they find his accomplice, too."

"Yes, well, it all has to be investigated. Is Amber still at her parents' house in Atlanta? I'm sure the police will want to talk to her again now that her attacker is dead."

"I don't think Amber wants to talk to anyone until she feels safe," Rachel said. "The other man is still out there, and he was dressed in a uniform, too. Until he's caught, I think she's going to stay under wraps."

"Of course," Officer Wilson said. "I don't blame her. But we don't have a statement on file from her yet."

"Agent Carver took her statement before she left," Rachel told her. "And we just spoke to him today. He's finally accepted that Amber's abduction could be connected to the murders and will be investigating Krigbaum. I was under the assumption that the police and FBI were working together on this case."

"Oh, yes, we are. Agent Carver just hasn't been very transparent of late. And like I said, I'm not involved with the Krigbaum death, so I'm not sure what was shared."

Rachel thought the officer sounded unsure of herself, although it could be because she wasn't being kept abreast of the case.

"I just wanted to let you know about his death," Officer Wilson said. "I'm sure you'll feel safer now that he's no longer out there."

"Yes, I will. Thank you for calling," Rachel said before both women hung up.

Rachel turned to Jack. "Well, that was interesting. Officer Wilson wanted me to know that Krigbaum was dead but that she knew nothing about the case."

Jack thought a moment. "I suppose it went to the FBI since he abducted Amber. But I thought they were all working together to catch the killer or killers."

"I did too." Rachel sat on the sofa across from Jack. "Maybe we should keep looking into this ourselves."

Jack grinned. "I was hoping you'd say that. I thought I'd go to the airport and see if I could get a list of private planes that came in either Friday or Saturday after Amber was abducted. That could tell us a lot."

"Good idea. I'm going to search online for more information about the California and Florida murders. I might even try a background check on Danvers. Maybe he's been in trouble before."

"Okay." Jack stood and stretched. "I'll leave Captain with you. See you in a few."

As Jack walked out the door, Rachel couldn't help but smile. She liked Jack, and they worked well together. But she also felt a little guilty about spending so much time around him. She knew he liked her, and she didn't want to encourage that. Her relationship with Avery was going strong, and she didn't want to do anything to jeopardize it.

Rachel thought about calling Avery to fill him in on what had happened so far but then decided against it. She knew he'd be working long hours on his own case, and she didn't want to interrupt him. She'd wait until he called her.

"Come on, Captain," she said as she walked past the big dog. "Let's do some more research." Captain got up, stretched like Jack had done, and happily followed her to her office.

* * *

Rachel spent an hour on the computer until her back ached from sitting too long. She hadn't learned anything new about the cases, and her background check on Danvers came up clean. Maybe they were fooling themselves, thinking they could solve this case with the little information they had compared to the files upon files the FBI most likely had compiled. But the sooner it was solved, the sooner the girls could return to their lives.

Rachel took Captain outside in the backyard and stood out there for a while. She loved her quiet neighborhood and the privacy of her yard. What she didn't like was not feeling safe alone because of the kidnapper still at large. Finally, she called Captain in and locked the door behind her.

It was late afternoon, so Rachel looked in her refrigerator for ideas for dinner. There was leftover pizza, salad, and not much else. They'd have to order in or go out to eat dinner. As she pondered this, her phone buzzed. She smiled when she saw it was Avery.

"Hey, there," she said. "I wanted to call you, but I didn't want to bother you at work."

"Anytime you call would be a welcome distraction," he said warmly. "How are things going there? Anything new?"

"We're at a stalemate," Rachel said, sighing. "Agent Carver and Jonathan Danvers seem a little too cozy considering their paths crossed in California, too. No one knows anything about Krigbaum yet. And someone broke into the Johnstons' house but didn't steal anything, so we think they were searching for Amber."

"Wow. That's crazy. Are the girls still okay?" Avery asked.

"Yes. They're safe. But the second kidnapper is still at large, so we're not telling anyone where they are," Rachel said.

"Good. Keep it that way." He paused. "This case I'm working on has brought up an interesting lead. A young woman who disappeared from San Francisco a few years ago and was found dead here in Idaho was thought to be a victim of our killer here. But the more I study this case, the more I realize she doesn't fit the profile. The Idaho killer stays close to his own state. I don't think he'd go as far as San Francisco."

"How long ago was she murdered?" Rachel asked.

"Sometime around six years ago," Avery said. "At the same time the LA killer was making the rounds. And she was a college student. But why she was brought to Idaho is beyond me."

"That's interesting." Rachel pondered it a moment. "Did she have evidence on her that pointed to your serial killer?"

"No. In fact, she had nothing on her at all. It's like they'd made her shower and clean up, and her clothing had no rips or tears either. She was clean as can be. Yet, we know she was raped and then murdered. Her body was dumped on the side of the road in plain sight."

"That's exactly how the women here are found," Rachel said. "There's evidence of sexual activity, yet no DNA left on them. Whoever is doing this is making sure the murders aren't tied to him."

"The guy we're searching for here isn't that neat. He leaves the victims a mess, then dumps them in remote places. That's why I don't think this woman's murder is associated with this killer," Avery said. "Maybe I should send the information to Carver and see what he thinks. He worked on the California murders, so he might be interested."

"I think you should, too," Rachel said.

"How are you doing?" Avery asked, his tone softening. "I'm sure Julie's passing has been hard for you."

"It has, but with the murders here and my worrying about Amber and Jules' safety, I haven't had much time to process it. I set the funeral out a week. I wish you could be here."

"Text me the date and maybe I can fly there for it," Avery

said. "I want to be there for you and Jules. I wish I was there with you now."

Rachel smiled at her phone. "I do too, but you have a job to do. Once you find your serial killer, and we find ours, maybe we can go on a vacation that has nothing to do with murder."

"That would be a nice change," Avery said.

After they'd hung up, Rachel felt better. Avery always managed to lift her spirits.

As Rachel was getting a glass of ice water from the fridge, Jack unlocked the front door and came inside. He smiled at her across the room, and she smiled back. "You must have found something," she said. "You look happy."

"I did." Jack locked the door behind him. He headed for the kitchen counter and placed some papers on it.

"Do you want a soda or some water?" she asked.

"Sure. A Coke would be nice."

She brought him a can. "So, what did you find?"

"I spoke with a guy at the airport who fuels the private planes that come and go," Jack said. "Private planes don't have to register flight plans, so they pretty much come and go as they please. But he had a list of the types of planes that came in and left over the weekend and who the owners are because he charges the fuel to them."

"Did you recognize any names?" Rachel asked.

"Oh, yeah. Saturday afternoon, a four-seater came in that is owned by JRD Enterprises. He said they refueled and sat and waited for about two hours, then took off. Later that day, a larger, luxury private plane flew in carrying Johnathan Danvers. Danvers had a car waiting for him and left, and the plane refueled and parked."

"Who owns JRD Enterprises?" Rachel asked.

"Johnathan Reginald Danvers," Jack said. "I asked the guy if it was normal for JRD Enterprises to send in a small plane, and he said he'd filled it up a few times over the past few months." Jack pointed to the papers on the counter. "He looked up the dates for me and printed them out."

"Have you compared them to the dates when the women went missing?"

"Not yet," Jack said. "Do you want to do the honors?"

Rachel went to her office to get the sheets she had on the other women who'd been murdered. She brought them back and compared the dates with the flight dates. She was able to match dates of abductions with flights in and out. Then, there were flights that flew in a few days after each abduction. She looked up at Jack. "These are pretty damning. Is it enough to charge a person with murder?"

"Probably not, but it's some pretty incriminating evidence. Danvers would need a good excuse for his plane to be coming and going like that. And we don't know if they flew to his private island or somewhere else. But the FBI could get that information."

"But can we trust Agent Carver with this information?" Rachel asked. "He might be working alongside Danvers."

Jack nodded. "We need to do more digging. Maybe we should see what more we can find out about Krigbaum. He had to be getting paid by whoever he was abducting women for. There has to be a connection somewhere."

Rachel sat back in her seat. "I wish we knew who we could trust. There's only so much we can do on our own."

"Has there been any more information about Krigbaum on the news?" Jack asked.

Rachel shook her head. "Not that I've seen."

Jack gave her a mischievous grin. "What if we leaked some information to the media about Krigbaum. Like, how he's suspected of having abducted Amber Johnston."

"Really?" Rachel was shocked. "You'd do that?"

Jack shrugged. "Anonymously, of course. It might get this case out in the open. With reporters digging into his life, they could find all sorts of things—and connections."

"But it would put Amber in the spotlight, and then the media might go looking for her," Rachel said. That was the last thing she wanted to do.

"She's safe. The girls are staying put, and no one knows where they are," Jack said. "I really believe Krigbaum is the key to who's connected with the abductions and murders of these young women. And Agent Carver isn't pursuing the connection."

"Do you have anyone you can give that story to who you trust will keep your name out of it?" Rachel asked.

"I think I do. But I want to make sure you're okay with it. It might work—or it might blow up in our face," Jack said.

Rachel sat still, thinking of what he'd said. They needed to prove Krigbaum was abducting young women, possibly for Danvers. If the police or FBI weren't even looking into it, then what choice did they have?

"Let's do it," she said. "We know for sure Krigbaum abducted Amber, so it won't be a lie. We'll see what the media does with it."

"I'll make some calls," Jack said. He picked up his phone. "You might want to call Amber on the burner phone to let her know what we're doing."

Rachel nodded. She went to get one of the burner phones and made the call.

CHAPTER ELEVEN

Later that evening, the local media was all over the connection between the deceased university policeman and Amber Johnston's abduction. Jack and Rachel were shocked that they'd grabbed it and run with it so quickly.

After Jack had made the call to his contact and Rachel had warned Amber what they were doing, they'd gone out and bought take-out for dinner. By the time they were settled back in her house, eating, with the TV on low, the news had erupted with Krigbaum's story.

"How do they get these on so fast?" Rachel asked, shocked at what was being aired. News reporters were interviewing college students about Krigbaum and were also reporting on his entire life.

"They work faster than the police," Jack said, chuckling. "Because the media doesn't have to prove anything, they can basically report anything as long as they say 'allegedly.'"

A reporter had interviewed several young women who were in a local tavern.

"Oh, yes. We all knew Officer Krigbaum," one young woman said, rolling her eyes. "He was always stopping and flirting with the women on campus and saying to call him Officer Krig." The girl shuddered. "No one liked him."

"Jules said something similar, didn't she?" Jack asked Rachel. "I can't believe this guy was openly flirting with the women."

"Yeah. It's pretty creepy." Shivers ran up Rachel's spine. "To think this guy was around all these young women, searching for his next victim."

After eating, Rachel called Camille and Ray to tell them what was happening.

"We saw it explode on the news tonight," Camille said. "I wondered where their interest came from. Do you think this will help?"

"We're not sure, but at least someone is looking into this guy," Rachel told her. "And it'll force either the police or FBI to start digging into him, too. We have to find the second kidnapper. What if he gets a new partner and another woman is taken? That would be awful."

"I agree," Camille said. "It's crazy that so many young women have been killed, yet they still haven't a clue who's behind it."

"I'm sure Krigbaum and his partner were killing the women," Rachel said. "But who was paying them to do it? We need to find that person."

After hanging up, Rachel sighed. It had been a long day, and she was tired of everything that had been happening. She curled up on the living room sofa. "I wish this was all behind us," she told Jack. "I just want life to go back to normal."

He nodded. "I know what you mean."

She eyed him. "And don't you have a job you need to get back to?" Rachel laughed.

"Yes, I do. But I'm basically working while I'm here. We had a body in Panama City Beach, too, and if I can tie it to these crimes, it'll solve that case."

Rachel perked up. "Speaking of that, Avery called earlier. There was a woman murdered in Idaho about six years ago. She was a college student from San Francisco. They had originally thought she was a victim of the serial killer they're investigating in Idaho, but Avery thinks otherwise. He said the body was completely clean and just left on the side of the road. Sound familiar?"

Jack sat up. "Yeah, it does. But why Idaho?"

"I don't know. I should look into the area where she was found. There are a lot of big ranches where people have money. Maybe she was flown there, and instead of bringing her back, they dumped her."

"It wouldn't be unheard of," Jack said. "Some serial killers have victims all over. Somehow, all of this must tie in together."

"I should do a search of all the properties JRD Enterprises owns," Rachel said. She sighed. "But not tonight. Tomorrow. I'm completely exhausted."

"I agree," Jack said. "We've caused enough trouble for one day." He pointed to the news, and they both laughed.

Jack took Captain out before bed, and Rachel put the dishes in the dishwasher. Jack came back in and filled Captain's water bowl, then got a glass of water for himself.

"I'm glad you and Captain are here," Rachel said, leaning against the kitchen counter. "I feel safer with you both here."

"I'm glad we're here, too," Jack said. "Although, I'm becoming very domesticated living in this family unit." He chuckled.

"Nothing wrong with being domesticated," she said, smiling. She studied Jack a moment. He was a good-looking man, there was no argument about that, and a kind-hearted one, too. She knew he'd do just about anything to keep her safe. It was a good feeling, yet she knew she shouldn't be thinking that way about him. She pushed away from the counter and moved to leave the room.

Jack frowned. "What's wrong?"

"Nothing," she said quickly. "I'm just tired. I'm going to bed."

"Okay. Goodnight."

"Goodnight," Rachel said, hurrying down the hallway. As she closed her bedroom door, she told herself that she'd better be careful. Spending this much time with Jack wasn't going to help her relationship with Avery. With a sigh, she got ready for bed.

* * *

Rachel rose early the next morning, and her mind was already in a whirl as she showered and dressed. She wanted to research JRD Enterprises and also watch the news and see what reporters had come up with about Krigbaum.

Jack was in the kitchen already, making coffee, when Rachel entered. She was about to say good morning when her phone buzzed.

"What the hell did you two do?" a male voice yelled over the phone.

Rachel pulled it away from her ear and saw it was Agent Carver. She quickly put it on speaker. "Excuse me?"

"Don't you dare deny that you and Jack Meyers weren't the ones who tipped off the press," Carver yelled. "Now we have press from all over the country butting into our investigation and crawling all over town."

Jack walked closer to the phone. "And the problem with that is?"

"You know damn well what the problem is," Carver said. "With the press in the way, we can't investigate quietly. They're watching our every move."

"Why would you want this case to be quiet?" Rachel asked. "Several women are dead, and as far as the public is concerned, you have no suspects or leads. It's about time people start bothering you for answers."

"It's not just me they're looking for," Carver said. "Everyone wants to know where Amber is because they want to interview her. It's only a matter of time before the press finds her. Then you won't feel so smug."

"You can threaten us all you want," Jack said angrily. "But don't you dare threaten Amber. Otherwise, you'll have to deal with me."

Rachel was surprised at how angry Jack was. But she agreed with him. No one should bother Amber.

There was an audible sigh on the other side of the line. "I'm not threatening anyone," Carver said, his voice calmer. "I'm just as frustrated with this investigation as you two are. Until a DNA profile of Krigbaum comes back, my hands are tied. He could be the one who killed all these women, or he could have just been a patsy. Either way, he's dead, and no new women have been abducted. We may already have our killer."

"You know that's not true," Rachel said. "Krigbaum's accomplice is still out there. And whoever was paying them is out there, too. His death may have stalled the abductions, but I doubt it stopped them completely."

Carver sighed again. "Do you still believe these women

were trafficked first before being murdered? That's a far-fetched story. No one is going to believe it."

"Why are you so sure it's not true?" Jack asked. "Do you know something we don't?"

"I probably know a lot that you don't know," Carver said sharply. "That's why you need to back off and let me do my job."

"Well," Jack said. "While you're doing your job, you may want to get a report on all the private planes coming and going at Tallahassee airport. I got one yesterday, and the comings and goings of a small plane owned by JRD Enterprises coincides with the abductions and murders of your victims."

"What?" Agent Carver sounded shocked.

"You do know who owns JRD Enterprises, don't you?" Rachel asked. "Your good friend, Johnathan Danvers."

There was silence on the other end for several beats. "I'll check it out," Carver said roughly, then he hung up.

Jack turned to Rachel. "Looks like we made his day."

She laughed.

After breakfast, Rachel got to work researching properties owned by JRD Enterprises. She'd thought it would be difficult to find that information, but to her surprise, there were several articles on real estate and financial sites sharing everything Danvers owned. She printed out sheets of information on his businesses and properties, then went to the kitchen to share the information with Jack.

Jack was sitting at the kitchen counter doing his own search on his laptop. He turned when he saw Rachel enter. "Did you find anything?"

"I found a ton of information. Apparently, rich people don't mind if everyone knows what they own and what their net worth is. You're going to find this interesting."

She pointed out the businesses first. "Danvers owns fifteen different businesses. One of them is a small plane rental company. They have twenty-five small four and six-seater airplanes that people can rent to go places or to get practice time for their pilot's license. It's located in Miami."

"Wow. That means he has planes at his beck and call at any time of the day or night," Jack said.

"He does. Especially when he has two pilots who work for the company and fly people around or train other pilots," Rachel said. "That means he can have a plane in and out of an airport whenever he needs one."

"What about properties?" Jack asked.

"Oh, they get even more interesting," Rachel said. "He has his large sprawling mansion on his own island in the Bahamas, and a penthouse apartment in Miami and New York City. Also, houses in Washington, D.C., Long Island, and Texas. He sold his Malibu home years ago but owns a large house in a lavish neighborhood in San Francisco. And look at this." She pointed to the last house on the list. "He owns a five-hundred-acre ranch outside of Coeur d'Alene, Idaho."

Jack whistled low. "So, the murdered woman in Idaho could be connected to Danvers."

"We don't have enough proof, but circumstantial evidence is piling up on him," Rachel said. "There's one more thing. He owns three large condominium buildings in Panama City Beach right on the beach. He has a private apartment in the penthouse of one of them."

"Another connection to a murdered woman," Jack said. "If we could tie him or Krigbaum to the victim in my city, we could blow this case wide open."

"And Agent Carver can't stop you from investigating the woman's murder in your jurisdiction," Rachel said.

Jack's eyes lit up. "No, he can't."

"Okay. What's the first thing we need to do?" Rachel asked.

"I'll call my office in Panama City Beach and see what evidence there is for the murder of that college student," Jack said. "Maybe you can call Officer Wilson and see if she knows if any DNA samples were sent off to the lab from Krigbaum. Even if they aren't working the case, they may know something."

"Good idea. I'll call her right now," Rachel said.

Rachel called Officer Wilson, and she answered right away.

"Hello, Rachel," Officer Wilson said, sounding upbeat. "What can I do for you?"

"We were wondering if you'd know if DNA was sent in from Officer Krigbaum. And if the clothes I gave you were processed for fingerprints or DNA," Rachel asked.

"I'm sorry, but as I said before, I'm no longer on the Krigbaum case since the FBI took it over," Officer Wilson said. "And as far as I know, the evidence you gave me that belonged to Ms. Johnston was handed over to Agent Carver."

"Oh, okay." Rachel was confused. She wondered why Carver hadn't mentioned getting the evidence. "Well, thank you for everything you've done for us. We're very happy that Amber was able to come home safely."

"You're welcome. I wish they would have let me be more involved, but the FBI trumps our department, unfortunately," Officer Wilson said. "I'm sure it will be weeks before they learn about any DNA connections if they exist. The labs are overrun with samples every day."

"Yes. I believe that," Rachel said. After she hung up, she turned to Jack, who'd just finished his call. "Officer Wilson said that Agent Carver has all the evidence now. Should I call him?"

Jack chuckled. "Maybe we should let him cool off first."

"I suppose you're right. I feel like our hands are tied. There's not much more we can do. And unless Agent Carver believes us about Danvers being involved, we're stuck."

"Yeah," Jack said. "And if Carver and Danvers are in cahoots, then nothing will get done."

Rachel sighed. "This is crazy."

"I was told I could pick up the evidence we have on the Panama City Beach murdered woman," Jack said. "We could drive over there for the night and come back tomorrow." He grinned. "Want to go on a road trip?"

Rachel laughed. "Sure. Why not? I wish we could visit the girls, but we might end up leading the killer right to them."

"Yeah. It's best to keep them invisible for a while longer," Jack said. "Pack a bag, and I'll buy you lunch on the way."

An hour later, they were on the road to Panama City Beach. Captain was curled up in the back of the SUV while Jack and Rachel sat in front.

"He's a good traveler," Rachel said, glancing back at Captain. "It's a good thing you have a big vehicle."

"Yeah. I've been driving him around since he was a pup. He's good company," Jack said.

"Better than me?" Rachel grinned.

"Oh, no. You're much better company," Jack said.

It took them two hours to reach Jack's house. He lived a few blocks from the police station in a nice little development with cozy-looking homes.

"This is nice," Rachel said as they entered through the side door into the kitchen.

"Not what you expected?" Jack asked, brows raised.

"I didn't know what to expect," Rachel said. "A single guy with a dog—it could have gone either way."

Jack chuckled. "My mother raised a neat freak. At least I try to keep things nice."

Rachel walked through the open kitchen, past the large island, and into the living room. It had a cathedral ceiling with dark beams and large windows facing the front of the house. "It's beautiful. And this fireplace." Rachel admired the stone structure that went up to the top of the high ceiling. "I love it."

"Thanks," Jack said, smiling proudly. "I'll show you to your room."

She followed him down a hallway toward the back of the house to a good-sized room that overlooked a lush backyard. "This is nice," she said, setting her overnight bag on the queen-sized bed. "Beautiful yard."

"Well, it's not as big as yours, but I like it. There's enough room for Captain to run around," Jack said. "I'd love to put an enclosed pool back there, but that costs quite a bit."

"You're not that far from the ocean, are you?" Rachel asked.

"It's a few blocks away, so I have to drive. But Captain and I go there most mornings to run."

"I'd love to live near the beach," Rachel said. "But I also love my place, so I doubt I'll ever move."

"Not even if you and Avery get married?" Jack asked.

Rachel felt a blush creep up her cheeks. "I don't think we're close to that yet. Even so, since he goes all over the country, I'd probably stay in my place."

"Ah. Sure. I don't blame you," Jack said. They were quiet for a moment, and Rachel felt a little awkward talking about Avery without him here.

Jack changed the subject. "Do you want to come to the office with me, and we can go through the evidence there? Then we can go to a place near the beach and have dinner."

"That sounds good," Rachel said, happy to talk about anything else besides her love life. "Let me change quick, and I'll be ready to go."

A few minutes later, Rachel felt refreshed in a clean pair of jeans and a blouse. She put on a touch of makeup and some short-heeled shoes that looked a little dressier. When she entered the kitchen, Jack was just putting dinner down for Captain. Jack had changed too, and Rachel caught the scent of a spicy aftershave in the air.

"Ready?" Jack asked.

"Yes," Rachel said. They hopped in the car and drove the few blocks to the police station.

When they entered, the officers sitting in cubicles they passed on the way to Jack's office were ribbing him. "Hey, you finally came into work," one guy said. "I thought you'd retired," a female officer told him with a chuckle.

"Funny," Jack said as he passed them. He had Rachel wait in his office while he retrieved the evidence box and shut the door when he returned. "They're all nosey around here," he said, placing the box on his desk.

Rachel laughed. "Well, you have been gone awhile."

"We were working," he said, then grinned.

Jack opened the banker's box, but it contained very little. There was a thin folder with the sparse information they had on the murdered woman, her clothing in plastic bags, and samples of DNA taken from underneath her fingernails. Her clothing had been free of evidence, and the DNA that had been processed didn't match any in the nationwide database.

Just like the women in Tallahassee, there was very little to trace back to anyone.

"She was a pretty young woman, just like the other Florida victims," Rachel said, studying her photo from her senior year in high school.

"Do you think Danvers would have had his minions come all the way over here to kidnap her? It seems unlikely," Jack said. "Unless Danvers was staying at his penthouse on the beach."

"Or someone he knew was staying there," Rachel said.

Jack's brows furrowed. "Meaning?"

"Maybe these college women weren't picked up for Danvers' pleasure but for his friends. Rich men who'd pay him for the girl of his choice."

Jack nodded. "Which is probably what is happening to the young women being abducted in Tallahassee. But why would a rich guy like Danvers want to do such a thing? He doesn't need the money."

"Maybe he uses the women to close deals. Or as a perk for working with him." Rachel said. "Even if it's not Danvers and we're way off, someone is moving these women out of Florida for the weekend and then bringing them back. Why else is there no sign of them, and then they appear a few days later?"

"I agree with that. But why not grab young women in a bigger city where they might not be missed right away? Tampa, Daytona Beach, or Miami? Why take college women who will be immediately missed?" Jack asked.

Rachel shook her head. "I don't know. Maybe it's some crazy fetish. Or maybe because it's fairly easy to move these women, unseen, in and out with private planes in Tallahassee. There must be some reason."

"Let's grab some dinner, and we can think about it," Jack

said. He closed the box and placed it on the table behind his desk.

A phone buzzed in Rachel's purse, and she dug inside for it. It wasn't her regular phone—it was the burner phone she'd been using to talk to Jules and Amber. "Hello?"

"Mom?" Jules sounded panicked. "Are you with Jack? There's something strange going on here."

"Yeah, Jack is here with me. What's happening?" Rachel put it on speaker.

"For the past two hours, a small, black van has been parked across the street from the house," Jules said. "It's freaking Amber out because it looks like the van she was abducted in. There's a guy in the driver's seat, just sitting in there. We think he's watching the house."

Jack spoke up. "You two stay inside and make sure everything is locked. Check that the security cameras are on, too. If you can get a photo of the van's license plate, then try, but don't let him see your faces. Your mom and I are here in town, so I'll have a patrol car follow us there to check it out."

"You're in town?" Jules asked, surprised.

"Yeah. It was a quick trip," Rachel said. "Just stay calm and safe. We'll be there in a few minutes."

"Okay," Jules said. "Hurry."

Rachel clicked off the phone as they both hurried out of the office.

"I need a patrol car to meet me at this address," Jack wrote it down for the officer sitting at one of the desks. "Can you call it in? There's a strange car stalking my mother's house."

"Sure thing," the officer said, already radioing for a car.

"Let's go," Jack said, and they hurried to his car.

CHAPTER TWELVE

Jack and Rachel jumped in his car and hurried through traffic.

"How on earth did they find the girls here?" Rachel asked.

"I don't know," Jack said angrily. "They must have done a search on me and found where my mother lived. That's how desperate these people are to make sure Amber doesn't talk. What the idiot in the van doesn't know is that Amber can't describe him anyway."

It wasn't long before they pulled into his mother's neighborhood and made it to the house. The patrol car was right behind them. Just as Jules had said, there was a small, black van sitting across from the house.

Jack pulled into his mother's driveway as the patrol car stopped behind the van. "Stay in the car," he told Rachel. "This guy could be armed."

Jack grabbed his gun out of the glove compartment and holstered it, then headed outside. Rachel watched as he and the patrol officers approached the van. Suddenly, the van door swung open, and a portly man jumped out and ran toward the house next door to Jack's mother's house. The officers ran after him, shouting for him to stop. The man turned and shot at the officers, then ran between the houses and away through the dark neighborhood.

Jack raised his hand to the officers to not shoot back and not follow. Rachel watched with relief. The last thing she wanted was to see Jack and the officers have a shootout with that guy in a neighborhood of families.

Jack came back to the car. "He must have been guilty of something because he ran off."

"I'm glad you didn't chase him," Rachel said. "If he's Amber's abductor, he wouldn't hesitate to kill you."

Jack grinned. "I'm glad you're worried about my welfare."

She rolled her eyes. "Don't get cocky, Lieutenant."

He laughed.

One of the officers came up to him. "The van is leased to a Carl Krigbaum of Tallahassee," he said. "Isn't that the officer who was found dead on the side of the highway?"

Jack nodded. "It was. Let's get this van to the garage so it can be searched for evidence. If we're right about it, they were abducting our murder victims in it."

"Yes, sir," the officer said.

"And could you and your partner stay here until we get the young women from this house out safely?" Jack asked the officer. "That guy knows they're here, and we need to find them a new safe house."

The officer looked surprised but nodded. "Of course."

Jack turned to Rachel. "Let's go get the girls."

Jules and Amber were thrilled to see Jack and Rachel when they walked into the house. The girls hugged them both.

"I'm so glad you two were in town," Jules said. "When we

first noticed the van, we didn't think much of it, but as it grew dark and it was still there, we freaked out. Was it the guy who abducted Amber?"

"We don't know who it was," Rachel said. "But he ran, so he's guilty of something. The van is leased to Krigbaum, so it has to be his partner."

Amber wrapped her arms around herself. "I can't believe he found us. I'm so glad you were able to come so soon. Just think, he could have broken in and taken me again."

Rachel placed her arm around Amber. "I'm glad we were here, too. He's not going to get you, I promise. We'll have to find a new place for you to stay."

"I've never seen his face, but I guess he doesn't know that," Amber said, sitting on the sofa. "Until they catch him, I'm not going to feel safe anywhere."

Rachel felt so helpless. She knew Amber was right, but she wasn't sure what they could do. At this point, they didn't trust anyone to protect her.

"You'll be safe with us for now," Jack said. "Why don't you pack up, and we'll head back to my house. Then we can call your parents, Amber, and see what they think."

The girls went to pack their bags while Jack walked into the kitchen to start the dishwasher and clean up. He didn't want his mother to come home to a mess. Rachel followed him in there.

"I don't think Amber had mentioned it was a black van before," she said. "I remember she said it had no windows in the back." She frowned as she tried to remember something.

"What is it?" Jack asked, watching her.

"Something about a black van. I remember seeing one, but I can't quite place where or when." She shook her head. "Maybe

I'm just losing my mind."

Jack chuckled. "I highly doubt that. But I'm not sure when you would have come across the van before. They're all over the highway, though. You may just remember seeing one."

"Maybe," Rachel said. But it bothered her.

Rachel went into the girls' bedroom, took the sheets off the bed, and loaded them into the washing machine. She replaced the comforter and pillows and helped the girls fold clothes for their bags.

Once the girls were packed, Jack moved the SUV closer to the back door so they could get in without being seen. He put their bags in first, then stood guard while the girls got in the back seat. Once they were safely in the car, Jack walked out to tell the officers they were leaving and thank them for helping. The tow truck was already there to bring the van into headquarters.

"I'll get you all home safely and then go out and pick up some dinner," Jack said as he drove toward his house. "Captain will protect you."

Rachel laughed. "Captain sure works hard."

"He does," Jack agreed.

"If that guy knows where your mother lives, he must know where you live," Amber said nervously. "What if he comes there tonight?"

"Good point," Jack said. "I'll call the department and see if we can get a patrol car to sit outside the house. I'm sure we'll be fine, though. That guy knows we're on to him, and he doesn't have a car now, so he's going to want to get out of town."

Rachel was relieved that they had Jack with them. If she'd had to deal with all this alone, she'd be scared out of her wits. Especially since they had no one else they could trust.

Once they arrived at Jack's house, he escorted the girls and Rachel inside before getting the luggage. He gave them the room next to Rachel's.

"I'm going to check all the doors and windows, just to make sure they're locked. I have cameras outside the house, so we should know immediately if anyone trips one," he told them. "We'll be fine here for the night."

While the girls settled in, Jack called for a squad car to sit outside his house and was able to get one. Then he asked everyone what they wanted for dinner.

"Anything except pizza or pasta," Jules said. "We've been eating a lot of frozen dinners, and we're sick of them."

Rachel laughed. "I'm sure we can order something a little healthier."

They settled on food from a place Jack knew of that made great shrimp and grilled chicken salads. He called in the order, and when the patrol car showed up, he headed out to get the food. They all sat at the counter in the kitchen when he returned and enjoyed the food.

Amber had called her parents by then to let them know what was happening. "My mom thinks I should come home. She figures I'd be safe there now. But it's only three more days until we start back to school."

"Unless they solve this case, I don't think it'll be safe for you to go back to the college yet," Rachel said. "Maybe you can work online for a while."

"I don't know," Amber said. "I really don't want to miss classes, but I don't feel safe there, either. At least not until that guy is found."

"What about me?" Jules asked. "I need to return to school on Monday, too."

"I don't feel safe with you on that campus either," Rachel said.

"We can't hide forever," Jules said. "Krigbaum is dead, and the other guy is on the run. And they aren't looking for me."

"No," Jack said. "They aren't, but you live with Amber. You aren't safe either."

Jules sighed. "I hate this. I wish they'd just solve the case."

"Don't we all," Rachel said.

"The good news is because this happened in my district, I can now officially work on this case," Jack said. "And we have the van, so I can request the reports on Amber's clothing and anything else found from the other murders to test against what we find in the van. If we can match even one fiber from Amber's clothing to the van, we can officially say that Krigbaum was involved and work our way backward."

"That's great," Rachel said. "I've also been thinking about how we can tie Danvers to these killings. Did you notice if the airport had outdoor security cameras where the private planes come and go?"

"No, I didn't notice. But I can call the fuel guy and ask," Jack said, suddenly intrigued.

"If they keep any of their footage in the cloud for months, we might be able to get video of them bringing one of the victims to the plane or from the plane," Rachel said. "And if the plane belongs to Danvers, we'll have him."

"I'll get on that right away tomorrow," Jack said. "Should I give our friend, Agent Carver, a call and let him know we have the van or just wait a while?"

"Let's wait," Rachel said. "If he's able to get it from you, then you won't have a chance to search it."

"He won't be happy that we're withholding evidence," Jack

said, grinning.

"Too bad."

They both chuckled. They knew the FBI would take it even-tually, but it was important to get evidence while they could.

* * *

The next morning, they decided to stay an extra day at Jack's house so he could oversee the collection of evidence inside the van. The police were still searching for the guy who'd run, but so far, they had no leads. Rachel, Jules, and Amber stayed at the house while Jack went to work, and a patrol car was parked in front of the house for their safety.

Rachel was happy to spend some time with her daughter and Amber after everything that had happened. She'd hated sending them away, but it had been for their own protection. Now, Rachel realized that no one was ever safe if someone was intent on finding them.

Around noon, Jack called Rachel. "I talked to Agent Carver about getting the report from Amber's clothing, and he said he didn't have the bag of clothes. Didn't Officer Wilson tell you she'd handed the clothes over to him?"

"Yeah, she did. That's weird." Rachel wondered why she would have said it if it wasn't true. "How did Agent Carver respond to you having Krigbaum's van?"

"He immediately claimed it, but when I told him Amber was in my district when we confiscated it, he backed down," Jack said. "And to be fair, I said I'd share any evidence I find with him. This van could crack the case wide open, so we have to work together. Carver calmed down after that, but I did promise to send the van to him once we'd gone over it."

"That's good," Rachel said. "We don't need him as an enemy."

"Also, you wouldn't believe our luck," Jack said, sounding excited. "There were empty coffee cups on the floor of the van. We can get DNA from them. Maybe they'll lead us to the guy who ran off last night."

"That would be great," Rachel said.

"I was wondering if I could send a female officer over to the house to collect DNA and hair samples from Amber. Do you think she'd be okay with that?" Jack asked.

"If it'll help find the murderers, I'm sure she won't mind. Why don't you send someone over, and I'll talk to Amber. If she's against it, I'll let you know."

After hanging up, Rachel approached Amber. "Would you mind giving a DNA and hair sample to the police? They could use it for their investigation of the van."

"Sure," Amber said. "I'll do whatever it takes to find that guy and get him off the streets."

Rachel was happy she'd agreed. It wouldn't be too far-fetched to find hair samples from all the girls in that van unless they'd been fastidiously cleaning it.

A female police officer came and swabbed Amber's mouth. She also took hair samples and her fingerprints. "If we find any evidence you were in that van, we'll know we have the right person," the officer said. After she left, Amber seemed downhearted.

"What's wrong?" Jules asked her friend.

"Giving my DNA and fingerprints almost makes me feel like a criminal," Amber said. "I wish they'd catch the guy so we can move on with our lives."

"I'm sorry, dear," Rachel said, hugging her close. "I can see why you'd feel that way. But it's the only way to get proof that they used that van to abduct you and the other girls."

"I know," Amber said. "I'm just so sick of all this. I know I'm lucky to be alive, but as long as I have to be in hiding, it feels like I'm still a captive."

"I totally understand," Rachel said. Rachel had kept a low profile a couple of years before when she became the center of attention on the news after learning her hometown thought she was the little girl in the grave from decades earlier. "Hopefully, it will be over soon."

Jack returned that evening with a bag full of Mexican food for dinner and good news. "We found a lot of evidence in the van," he said happily. "Hair, fingernails, fingerprints. They must have never cleaned it out. They were so arrogant, I guess they thought they'd never get caught."

"That's great," Rachel said, happy to hear about the evidence. "But I suppose it'll take weeks to get results from the lab."

"It will," Jack said. "But I begged the lab to run the guy's DNA from the coffee cups as quickly as possible. I'm hoping he's in the system, and we can identify him."

"That would be great," Amber said. "I wish I'd seen his face, but he always wore a mask around me."

"I also talked to Agent Carver again, and he has DNA from the murdered women in Tallahassee. Once they process what was found in the van, it can all be compared." Jack grinned. "Not bad for only one day of work."

Rachel laughed. "You can pat yourself on the back—you did good."

As they ate dinner, they discussed what was next. "Tomorrow, we should go back to your home, and I can check the video footage at the airport," Jack said. "I didn't tell Carver that Amber would be with us. As far as anyone knows, she's still hiding somewhere."

"Will you feel safe at my house?" Rachel asked Amber. "Or would you rather go home?"

"I'd be just as safe at your house as at my parents' house," Amber said thoughtfully. "So, I'd rather stay with you. At some point, I'll have to return to college."

"We both need to," Jules said. "But it doesn't sound like this case will be solved in the next two days."

"We're doing our best," Jack said. "I wish we knew who we could trust. I should talk to Carver about closing the college campus another week until we can find the second guy. We really have no idea how many police are involved with the abductions."

"Or if Agent Carver is involved," Rachel said.

"Well, no matter what happens, we can go home tomorrow," Jules said. She leaned down and petted Captain on the head. "At least we know we can trust Jack and Captain."

Rachel laughed. "Yes. Captain is the most trustworthy of all."

"Hey," Jack said. "I take offense to that." But he was smiling.

"Okay," Rachel said. "We completely trust you, too."

Jack's phone rang, and he glanced down at it. "What on earth would Carver want this late at night?" He answered it.

"Well, you did it again," Agent Carver yelled over the phone.

Jack and Rachel stared at each other. What was wrong now?

CHAPTER THIRTEEN

"You managed to be on the ten o'clock news," Agent Carver said loud enough for everyone to hear. "So much for keeping a low profile."

Rachel grabbed the remote and turned on the news. A station in Panama City Beach was also running something about the black van and how it might be tied to the murders of the Tallahassee college girls as well as the girl in Panama City Beach.

Jack put the phone on speaker. "We didn't tell anyone at the news station. I suppose one of the officers from last night might have called it in, but I highly doubt it."

"How are we ever going to keep ahead of the murderers if the news keeps reporting everything we find?" Agent Carver sounded irritated. "I didn't have any trouble with the media until you two got involved.

"Settle down," Jack told Carver, annoyance lacing his voice. "The murderer knows we have his van—he shot at us and ran away from it. It really isn't news to him."

"It's the whole case," Carver said. "It's more than just one guy in a van. It's the ringleader or whoever else is involved at the top. Just make sure no more information gets out before we've had time to process everything."

"What do you mean, the ringleader?" Rachel asked. "I thought you were convinced this was a one-man serial killer doing the murders."

"I'm looking at all the leads," Agent Carver said. "Just keep everything to yourselves." He hung up before Jack or Rachel could reply.

"Hm," Rachel said. "Suddenly, he believes we might be right?"

"Who knows?" Jack said. "He doesn't believe in sharing, that's for sure."

That night they all went to bed feeling secure in the fact that Jack and Captain were locked inside the house with them and a patrol car was outside. The next morning, they packed their bags and headed out in Jack's car toward Tallahassee.

Along the way, Rachel called Officer Wilson to ask about Amber's clothing.

"I gave it to Agent Carver, like I told you," Officer Wilson said, sounding confused.

"Jack called him about it, and Carver said you never gave it to him," Rachel said. She was puzzled as to why either one of them would be lying.

"Well, we dropped it off at his headquarters," she said. "Maybe someone put it aside and forgot to give it to him."

"Does that happen?" Rachel asked, shocked. "Does evidence from an abduction generally get lost so easily?"

"No, of course not," Officer Wilson said. "But Agent Carver hasn't been the most congenial person. I'll call over there and see what I can find."

"I'd appreciate it," Rachel said.

"I saw the van was confiscated on the news last night," Officer Wilson said. "And the guy shot at the police. Did anyone get a good look at him before he got away?"

"No, unfortunately not," Rachel said. "But we have his DNA, so it's only a matter of time."

"Has Amber remembered anything more about the guy?" Officer Wilson asked.

"No. Nothing more than she's told us," Rachel replied. She thought it was strange that Officer Wilson was so interested in the guy. "Have you or Agent Carver come up with anything new?"

"I don't know about Agent Carver," she said. "But I'm not working the case, so I know nothing new. I'm glad Jack can officially work on it. Maybe you'll get more answers that way."

"We're hoping to," Rachel said. She hung up, feeling slightly confused about her conversation with Officer Wilson.

"What is it?" Jack asked, glancing over at her.

"Officer Wilson wondered if we got a good look at the suspect from the van. I'm just a little baffled why she'd ask that," Rachel said.

"Maybe she's secretly still looking into the case. She seemed like a good investigator," Jack said.

"Maybe," Rachel said. Still, she wondered about the officer.

Throughout the drive, Jack watched the traffic around them to make sure they weren't being followed. And once they were back at Rachel's place, Jack searched the house and yard before the women got out of the car and went inside. They didn't want to take any chances that someone might try to get Amber.

"Now what?" Rachel asked. "Should we trust Agent Carver and ask for a patrol car to be parked outside the house? Or maybe Officer Wilson?"

"I'm not sure," Jack said. "Even if both Agent Carver and Officer Wilson are clean, another person around them could be part of this abduction case. Maybe it would be best if no one knows Amber's with us."

Rachel sighed. "We have no choice. At least I have the cameras around the house, and we have Captain for protection."

Jack raised his brows. "And me."

She chuckled. "And you, of course."

The girls settled in, and Rachel made lunch for everyone. After they ate, Jack said he was going to the airport to check if they had cameras in the private plane area.

"I'll go with you," Rachel said. "If there is footage to look at, two people can get through it faster than one."

Jack nodded. "Will you both feel safe alone here?" he asked Jules and Amber.

"We'll be fine," Jules said. Amber nodded.

Jack and Rachel left, leaving Captain with the girls. It took them half an hour to get to the airport, and they parked near the fence where the private hangars were located. A small building sat to the side, and when they entered, a young woman behind the counter smiled at them.

"Are you here to rent a plane?" she asked.

"No," Jack said. "I wanted to ask a few questions about the facility." He flashed his badge, and the woman's expression grew serious.

"Oh, yeah. Sure. But weren't you guys already here asking questions?" she said, looking confused. "Someone from the FBI was here a few days ago."

Jack looked at Rachel, then back at the woman. "This is a follow-up. Do you know if there are cameras outside where the planes are parked and around the hangars?"

"Yeah," she said. "We have cameras all over the yard. "Let me call Jake, and he can show you where they are." She radioed Jake and asked him to come inside. A few seconds later, the fuel truck man Jack had met before came through the back door that led to the runway and planes.

"Oh, hey," he said, recognizing Jack. "You're back again."

"Yeah. Hi, Jake. This is Rachel. She's helping me with the case," Jack said.

Jake nodded to Rachel. "So, what can I do for you today?"

"I'd like to see where you have outside cameras," Jack said. "If you don't mind showing me."

"Sure. Follow me." Jake turned and walked out the door, with Jack and Rachel following. Jake led them around the yard, pointing out cameras on the corner of the building that faced the runways and more cameras on each hangar. There were two cameras facing different directions toward the area where planes were tied down when not in use.

"Do you know if they keep the video from these cameras in the cloud and for how long?" Jack asked Jake.

He grinned. "I'm actually in charge of the video and the cameras, too. I'm kind of a one-man show around here. We keep three months of video in the cloud before making room for new video, although no one ever looks at it."

Jack studied the young man. "Since you're around here full time and you fuel the planes, maybe you've noticed some strange stuff going on. Have you ever seen a small, black van with two guys park near the private planes and escort a young woman to one of the planes? Possibly a plane owned by Johnathan Danvers?"

Jake looked wary. "I haven't seen a black van around here,

but if one is coming in for the Danvers' plane, it would be at the rear hangar that I can't see from here. There are cameras back there, though. They would have caught something."

"Would it be okay if we go through the videos?" Jack asked. "We know what dates we're looking for, so we can narrow it down."

"Well, I'd have to call the manager and ask if it's okay," Jake said. "But since it's police business, I'm sure he will be fine with it. He is very clear about being transparent around here."

"Great. We can wait while you call."

Jake walked away from them and made his call in private.

Rachel whispered to Jack. "Do you think he's actually calling his manager or tipping off Danvers?"

Jack shrugged. "Who knows with this case. He could be calling Agent Carver, for all we know. But he seems like he wants to help."

Jake came back. "He okayed it. I'll show you where the laptop is, and you can scan through whatever dates you need to."

Jack and Rachel smiled. Hopefully, they'd find something.

Jake led them to a small room that was more like a closet. The laptop sat on a mini desk that only one person could sit at. "All the cameras are wireless," Jake said. He showed them how to find each camera and how to look through the history. He also showed them how to save a video and send it to email.

"Thanks so much," Jack said. He moved to let Rachel sit in front of the computer.

"If you need anything, holler," Jake said. Then he took off.

"Well, let's see what we can find." Rachel pulled out her phone and looked at the calendar. "We know that the last girl abducted before Amber was Melanie Lopez. She was found on March 11th, nine days after she'd been abducted. So that puts us at March 2nd. Which camera should we start with?" she asked Jack.

Jack stood behind her and pointed to the one showing Danvers' hangar. "Let's look at that hangar. If they brought her there, we'd see the black van drive in."

Rachel clicked on each video for that day. There were several since the cameras had motion detectors and people walked by or cars drove around all day long. After about an hour, Rachel realized it would take them a long time to watch videos for each day they needed to research.

Jack went to get them each a water from a vending machine down the hall, and when he returned, Rachel was excited.

"Look! This van pulled up to Danvers' hangar around five in the afternoon." They both watched as it backed up to the side door. Two men got out, opened the hangar's door, then opened the doors at the back of the van. Unfortunately, they couldn't see what or who was being unloaded.

"Is that the black van's license plate?" Rachel asked, looking up at Jack.

He pulled out his notepad and looked. "Yes, it is." Jack grinned. "We've got them!"

They continued to watch the video as the camera turned on and off. Only one man walked out of the hangar and headed to the driver's seat. He was heavier than the other man had been, but both had made sure to wear sunglasses and hats so Rachel couldn't see their faces. He drove away from the hangar. A few minutes later, someone else approached the hangar and opened the large, garage-style door. The small plane was unhooked from its tethers and pulled out of the garage.

"I can't tell if the thinner guy is sitting in the back of the plane with someone," Rachel said. "The windows are so small."

"Yeah. But it's a four-seater, so there's room for two passengers in the back," Jack said. "I wish we could see better, though."

The pilot pulled the plane out to face the airstrip, then walked around it, checking various parts of the airplane. After that, he closed the large garage door and got in behind the wheel. Several videos later, the airplane rolled between the hangars toward the runway. That was the end of the video.

"Krigbaum must have been in the airplane with Melanie in the back seat," Rachel said. "Even though we didn't see her, this proves that Krigbaum and the other guy were at the airport and loaded something into Danvers' plane. I wonder if there's a way to find out where that airplane was going?"

"Why don't you copy and download those last videos, and I'll ask the woman behind the counter if she has a record of the airplane's destination," Jack said.

As Rachel sent each video to her email address, she couldn't help but stare at the black van and driver as it drove away from the hangar. Something about it triggered a memory, but she just couldn't figure out why.

Jack came back, looking disappointed. "The private airplanes don't log their destinations with the office. That plane could have been going anywhere."

Rachel was disappointed too, but there wasn't anything they could do. "We should take this evidence to Agent Carver. He needs to know that van was connected to Danvers' plane."

Jack nodded. "Let's meet up with him now. We should come back tomorrow to look for more evidence. I hate leaving Amber and Jules alone this long."

"I agree." Rachel called Agent Carver's number and was glad when he answered. "We have something we need to show you," she told him.

An audible sigh came through the line. "Fine. Okay. Come to headquarters, and I'll talk to you." He gave her the directions to his office and hung up.

"He sounded happy," Rachel said, rolling her eyes.

"Well, you know how much he likes us," Jack teased.

They drove to an office building near the police station. On the way, Rachel called Jules to check up on them.

"We're fine," Jules said. "Just stir crazy. A week of being locked up is getting hard."

"Sorry," Rachel said. "But I think we're getting closer to ending this."

"I hope so. I know Amber would be a lot happier then," Jules said.

Rachel hung up as they pulled into the FBI headquarter's parking lot. When she and Jack entered the building, they were immediately stopped by a man in a black suit.

"Let them in," Agent Carver said, coming to the door. "They're here to see me." He waved for them to follow him. On the way to his private office, they passed a large room with a map on a cork bulletin board that had multiple pins on it and pictures of each of the victims. Several men and women were working at desks around the room.

Agent Carver led them to a smaller room where his desk sat. He walked around it and sat as he waited for them to take the seats in front. "Okay. What do you have now?"

"You sound so enthused," Rachel said sarcastically.

Jack chuckled. "We have video evidence that the black van registered to Krigbaum was connected to a plane owned by Jonathan Danvers."

Agent Carver sat forward at his desk. "Show me."

Rachel pulled out her phone and brought up the series of

videos. She handed her phone to Carver.

Agent Carver sat silent for a few minutes, going through each one. Then he handed her phone back. "All this shows is they went to the hangar, and then the airplane left. There's no proof they brought a woman there, and you can't see who's in the plane."

"This video was taken the same day Melanie Lopez was abducted," Rachel said. "We know Krigbaum was abducting girls—Amber identified him as one of her kidnappers. The fact that the van went to the airport, unloaded something, and the airplane took off proves that he and Danvers were connected."

"It still hasn't been proven that Krigbaum was abducting and killing girls," Agent Carver said. "All we have is Amber's identification. We won't have any proof until we find Amber's DNA, hair, or fingerprints in Krigbaum's van. Everything is up in the air until there's solid evidence to support it."

"So, you don't believe Amber?" Rachel asked.

"I believe she was abducted, but I have no physical evidence that she was in Krigbaum's van," Carver said. "And you can't go after Danvers just because someone used his airplane. It may have been rented. Who knows?"

"Then you should ask him," Jack said.

Agent Carver sat up straight. "I can't go after a guy as important as Danvers without physical evidence. I'm not even sure your theory makes sense. We're still looking for a serial killer, not some rich guy taking girls and then bringing them back to kill them."

Jack glared at Carver. "I'm beginning to think you're protecting this guy. Maybe you were protecting him in California all those years ago, too."

Agent Carver stood suddenly, propelling his chair back

against the wall. "You'd better have proof to back up that kind of accusation. And don't bother me again unless you have real proof."

Rachel stood and walked out, with Jack following her. They didn't speak until they were in the car.

"What a jerk," Jack said, fuming. "This is enough evidence to bring Danvers in."

"We'll just have to keep scanning the video until we find one of the murdered women on it," Rachel said. "If the van shows up at the airport each time a woman was abducted, he'll have to check into it."

Jack sighed. "Maybe. I'll go again tomorrow and see what I can find. Let's pick up dinner and bring it home for the girls."

"Sounds like a plan," she said, giving him a smile.

They ordered and picked food up, then drove the half-hour back to Rachel's house. As they approached the cul-de-sac and turned toward Rachel's driveway, she froze. "Oh, my God!" Rachel yelled.

CHAPTER FOURTEEN

"What?" Jack stomped on the brakes and looked all around him.

She turned to Jack. "I remember what I saw. I think I saw the other man's face from the black van."

"How?" Jack asked, totally confused.

"The evening Jules and I went to the first search for Amber. As I pulled up to the end of my driveway, I had to stop because a small black van was circling the cul-de-sac. The guy in the van looked straight at me."

"But why would they be here?" Jack asked.

"I don't know. I have to talk to Amber again about when she ran off. If it was after she'd run from them, they might have been checking the area." Rachel was excited now. She could see the guy's face as plain as day. At the time, she hadn't thought it was important, but now, it all fell into place.

Jack drove up to the house, and Rachel hurried inside, calling for Amber.

"What's up?" Amber asked, coming down the hallway from Jules' room.

"I need to confirm the timeline of what happened to you," Rachel said. She waved Amber over to sit on the sofa, and Jules and Jack followed suit. "You were abducted sometime before noon on Saturday. Do you know when you were able to escape?"

Amber thought about it. "I know I slept in the van overnight because at one point when I woke up the first time, it was dark out. Then the next day was when I pretended to be drugged even though I was awake. So, it would have been late afternoon on Sunday when I escaped because a few hours later, it was dark, and I hid."

"And you were north of Tallahassee?" Rachel asked.

"Yes, although I didn't know that until the next day," Amber said. "Why? What's up?"

Rachel smiled and looked over at Jules. "Remember the first night we went on the search for Amber in the field?" Jules nodded. "As I left the driveway, I saw that black van drive by. I wondered who they were but then forgot all about it. The man looked right at me. It wasn't Krigbaum, it was the other guy. I know what he looks like."

Amber's face lit up. "That's wonderful. The sooner he can be identified, the sooner he'll be off the streets."

"Now, all we need to do is figure out who we can trust with this information," Rachel said.

"Let's eat and discuss it," Jack said. "I don't know about you guys, but I'm starved."

They sat at the counter and passed around the plates and food. Jack and Rachel told the girls about the video they'd found at the airport and how Agent Carver reacted.

"It's frustrating," Rachel said. "It's like he doesn't want to find the killer or killers. And according to Officer Wilson, he's no longer sharing with the local police. I don't know if we can trust him or if we can trust her."

Jack looked thoughtful. "Maybe we should meet with both of them at once when you give them the man's description. I would hope that one of them is honest."

"Officer Wilson seems reliable. She seemed professional at the searches for Amber. We have to trust someone," Rachel said, feeling frustrated.

"I agree you should meet with both," Amber said. "Like Jack said, one of them should be able to do something with the information."

"Tomorrow morning, I'll go back to the airport and scan through more videos around the dates of the womens' disappearances," Jack said. "You can call Officer Wilson and Agent Carver and ask to meet them both at the police station. Once you have an appointment set, I'll meet you there, too."

"That sounds like a good plan," Rachel said. "I wonder if Danvers is still in Florida or if he's left for his island in the Bahamas?"

"Hopefully, he's still in the state. If I find anything tomorrow at the airport, I certainly want that guy arrested," Jack said.

That evening Jules and Amber received an email alert on their phones that the college campus was going to stay closed one more week because of the recent murders and Amber's abduction.

"That's good to hear," Rachel said. "I'm glad they're taking this seriously."

"It's a relief for me," Jules said. "I don't want to get behind on my classes."

"Now you two can sit back and relax tomorrow," Jack said. "And so can I. I hated the thought that there's still a killer out there and school was going to open again."

Later that night, after everyone had settled in their rooms, Avery called Rachel. "Hey, there. Are you all still safe and sound?" he asked.

"Yes, we are," she said, smiling at the phone. "We found some video that ties the black van with Danvers' airplane. Agent Carver said it wasn't enough to do anything with, though, so Jack is going to try to get more video tomorrow."

"Unfortunately, you need specific proof to arrest someone as powerful as Danvers," Avery said.

"Yeah, I understand that. But guess what? I remembered seeing the black van in our neighborhood the night after Amber disappeared. I'm almost sure it was the kidnappers scouring all the neighborhoods for Amber. And I got a good look at the driver, who wasn't Krigbaum."

"That's great news," Avery said, excitement in his voice. "Have you told the police yet?"

"I'm going to call tomorrow. We decided to talk to the police and Agent Carver at the same time. Really, at this point, we aren't sure who's legit and who isn't."

"I have a DNA chart from the victim we found in Idaho who was from California. Maybe I should send it to Jack to compare with the abductors' DNA they find in the van," Avery said. "It's a long shot, but who knows what they'll turn up."

"Great idea," Rachel said. "I'm looking forward to this being over so we can talk about mundane things."

Avery laughed. "When has that ever happened?"

"I know," she said, laughing too. "Maybe we can take a vacation in a few months when you're able to take a break from work."

"I'd like that," he said.

After they'd hung up, Rachel lay on the bed thinking about

how crazy her life had been over the past week. She hoped they'd find the answers soon so life would be boring again. Boring was good.

* * *

The next morning, Jack and Rachel were up early while the girls slept in. They ate breakfast together and planned their day.

"Do you have your list of the dates each girl was abducted?" Jack asked her as they sipped coffee.

"I'll give you a copy before you leave," Rachel said. "What time should I try to get everyone to meet at the station?"

"Maybe noon or one? That way, I'll have time to dig through several months of the airport videos," Jack said.

Rachel gazed at him over her coffee mug. "We might actually get a break in this case by tonight. That'll be wonderful, won't it?"

"It will," he said. "Except then I'll have to go back to my side of the state, and I won't get to see you every day."

Rachel grinned. "Lucky you."

"No. Unlucky me," Jack said.

Rachel dropped her eyes.

"Hey. I'm sorry if I made you uncomfortable," Jack said gently. "I know we can only be friends. But I do enjoy spending time with you."

"I enjoy spending time with you, too." Rachel cleared her throat. "By the way. Avery called last night and wondered if he could send the DNA charts for the murdered woman in Idaho to you."

Jack turned serious again. "Sure. We might get a match if any of the abductors' DNA was found on that victim."

"I'll tell him to send it then," she said.

Jack stood and rinsed out his coffee mug. "Well, I'll run to the airport. Call me as soon as you have a time set. I'll leave Captain here for protection." He rubbed the dog's head as he said it.

"I might have to steal Captain away from you," Rachel teased. "I'm getting used to him being around."

Jack looked at her for a moment, then smiled. "I'm sure he'd like that."

Rachel suddenly wished she hadn't said it. Their conversation was getting too personal. "I'll call you after I talk to Wilson and Carver."

"Okay. See you soon." Jack headed out the door, and Rachel locked it behind him.

Rachel sighed. Being in close quarters with Jack was getting to her. He was such a great guy, and if she hadn't been dating Avery already, it would be easy to fall for him. But she loved Avery. She had to remember to keep her emotional distance from Jack. But it was hard.

It was nine-thirty by the time Rachel called Officer Wilson.

"Hi, Rachel," Officer Wilson said. "What can I do for you?"

"I was wondering if I could meet you at the station at noon or one today. I have some new information that might help find Krigbaum's accomplice," Rachel said.

"Really? That would be incredible. Can you tell it to me on the phone?" Officer Wilson asked.

"I'd rather meet with you. And I'd like to include Jack and Agent Carver in the meeting. I think this information would be beneficial to both agencies."

"I see," Officer Wilson said. "Did Amber remember something new?"

"No, but I did. Quite frankly, I remembered seeing the accomplice, so I'll be able to describe him," Rachel said. "But I'd like to meet with you and the others in person."

"This would be a big breakthrough," Officer Wilson said, sounding interested. "Yes. Let's meet at one o'clock here at the station."

"Great," Rachel said. "I'll see you then."

After she'd hung up, she called Agent Carver. "Are you available at one today? I'd like you to join us at the police station for a meeting. I have some new information."

"New information. About what?" Carver asked.

"About Krigbaum's accomplice," Rachel said. "But I want to tell you and Officer Wilson at the same time."

Agent Carver sighed. "Fine. I'll meet you there. But quite frankly, Officer Wilson isn't involved with this case, so I don't understand why we have to include her."

"Because I need to make sure both agencies are looking for this guy," Rachel said, irritated. "I don't want to just tell you and have you sit on it. You did hear that the college closed for another week, didn't you? If we don't get this second guy off the streets, the college won't be safe even a week from now."

"Yes, I know they closed down for another week," Agent Carver said snidely. "And I do want to get this accomplice, if for no other reason than to mark him off as an abductor and not our serial killer."

Rachel held back her angry response. "I'll see you at the police station at one," she said, then hung up.

"That guy is so aggravating!" she said aloud to the empty room.

Amber came down the hallway. "What guy?"

"Agent Carver." Rachel moved over to sit on the sofa. "He

still doesn't believe your abduction has anything to do with his serial killer case. It's so frustrating."

Amber sat in a chair across from her. "He's probably put himself in a corner with the little evidence he has and refuses to see it differently."

"You'd think he'd be thankful that people are giving him new information he can follow up on," Rachel said. "I would."

"Maybe he has his theories and doesn't want to show his hand," Amber said. "He might actually believe Danvers has something to do with all this but can't quite piece it together."

Rachel tipped her head and stared at Amber. "What do you think? You were trapped in that van with those two men, listening to what they were saying."

Amber took a deep breath. "I'm not sure what to think. I know someone else was involved because Krigbaum kept calling someone who seemed to be giving him directions. Someone was trying to get them to an airport to fly me out. There was definitely a third person. I never heard a name, though."

Rachel nodded. "You are a very brave young woman, you know that? After all you've been through, you must be completely drained."

Amber smiled. "Actually, I'm feeling better now that we're staying here instead of just me and Jules at that other house. I feel safer here with you and Jack and Captain, too." She smiled at the dog as he came over at the mention of his name.

"I'm glad you feel safe here," Rachel said. "And I hope we can finally get some closure and catch the other guy."

The three women stayed inside for the rest of the morning and had lunch before Rachel got ready to leave for the police station. She'd called Jack earlier to tell him the time they were meeting. He'd sounded very pleased with himself.

"I've found some great footage," he'd told her. "I can't wait to show this to Carver and see his reaction."

"That's wonderful," Rachel had said. "I just want this to be over."

"I'm sure a lot of people feel that way," Jack had said. "I'll see you soon."

Before leaving, Rachel put Captain outside in the backyard to do his business. She didn't want Jules or Amber to leave the house while she was gone. As she walked down the hallway from putting the dog out, she was surprised by a knock on the door. Amber and Jules were sitting at the kitchen counter, and they both froze.

"Why don't you go to the bedroom while I see who this is," Rachel whispered. The two young women hurried down the hallway.

Rachel peered out the living room window and was surprised to see Officer Wilson, in full uniform, standing at the door. Rachel looked around and saw the police car, but no one else was in it. She opened the front door slightly but kept the screen door shut.

"Hi," Rachel said to Officer Wilson. "We were supposed to meet at one at the station."

Officer Wilson nodded. She seemed distracted. "I know. I'm sorry to barge in like this. I was on patrol and decided to stop by. I'm not sure I would have been able to make it back to the station by one. Is it okay if we talk now?"

Rachel didn't move to open the door wider. "I really wanted to talk to you and Agent Carver together."

"I called Agent Carver, and he didn't care if I came early," Officer Wilson said. "He's a little annoyed by all of this anyway." She rolled her eyes. "Sorry, but you know how he is."

Rachel laughed, easing some of the tension she'd been feeling. "Yeah. That sounds like him."

"May I come in?" Officer Wilson asked.

Rachel had no reason to suspect her of any wrongdoing, and she seemed sincere. Making a quick decision to trust Officer Wilson, she opened the door wider. "Sure. Come on in."

Officer Wilson opened the screen door and walked inside. "Is Jack here?" she asked, glancing around. "Or your daughter?"

Rachel's suspicions rushed back. "Jack's coming back any minute to drive me to the station," she lied.

Captain began to bark wildly in the backyard.

"Then I guess we'd better do this quickly," Officer Wilson said, all pretense of friendliness gone. "Get in here!" she yelled out the screen door.

Rachel backed up as the screen door opened. In walked a short, round man in a police uniform with his gun drawn. Rachel recognized him immediately. It was Krigbaum's accomplice from the van.

CHAPTER FIFTEEN

"So, you do recognize my fellow officer," Officer Wilson said. "Of course, he doesn't really work for the police force, but I was able to get him a uniform as a disguise." She pulled her gun and waved at the man. "Randy, search the house. I don't want Jack coming out here with his gun, surprising us."

"I tried the back door, but that damn dog is in the back-yard," Randy said, sounding whiny.

"Just go," she snapped. As Randy hurried down the hall-way, Officer Wilson trained her weapon on Rachel.

Rachel glared at Officer Wilson. She couldn't believe she'd trusted her just moments before. Rachel knew she'd have to keep Wilson talking as she tried to figure out a way to get the upper hand. She spoke calmly. "Randy? That doesn't sound like a killer's name."

Officer Wilson laughed. "He was a paramedic when I met him in California. Would you also be surprised to know we're married?"

Rachel couldn't believe what she was hearing. "You've been a participant in the abductions all along?"

"Of course. I'm the brains. Krigbaum was an idiot, so we got rid of him," Officer Wilson said proudly. "He got sloppy."

"Get out there," Randy ordered from down the hallway. Captain was barking wildly through the screen door. Randy had his gun on Amber and Jules as they joined them in the living room. Rachel inched her way toward the girls and stood in front of them.

"So, we're all here," Officer Wilson said. "Good. I can get rid of all of you at once. But we have to be smart about this. Maybe make it look like a murder-suicide."

"No one would ever believe that," Rachel said. "And you and your friend are already on my security cameras."

"Oh, yeah. Thanks for reminding me," Officer Wilson said. "I'll get your phone after you're dead and erase them. Now, all of you, sit down."

Jules and Amber both sat on the sofa, but Rachel continued to stand in front of them. "You couldn't possibly be the head of this operation," Rachel said, trying to keep her talking. "There had to be someone with money paying you." Rachel's phone buzzed in her front pocket, and she pulled it out. Jack was calling. He probably wanted to know why she wasn't at the police station. She hit the button to answer just as Officer Wilson moved forward and knocked it out of her hands. It landed on the floor near Rachel's feet.

"No phone calls." Officer Wilson pushed her face into Rachel's and growled, "I said to sit down.".

Rachel slowly lowered herself between the girls on the sofa.

"So, you don't think I was smart enough to plan the abductions and killings?" Officer Wilson said. "Well, I did. And yes, I had money behind me. Why else would I do it?"

"Jonathan Danvers was funding the whole thing, wasn't

he?" Rachel said. "But why? Were you trafficking the women somewhere and then bringing them back to kill them?"

"Oh, you're so smart, aren't you?" Officer Wilson said sarcastically. "Danvers would ask for a certain type of girl, and we'd find her for him. It wasn't always for him, though. Sometimes he brought them to his island for his rich friends, who paid a lot of money for a night with the young woman of their dreams."

Rachel felt sick, but she had to keep Wilson talking. "Why did you bring the women back? Why not dispose of them in the Bahamas?"

"Because Danvers wanted it to look like a serial killer. That way, the Feds and cops couldn't tie it to him," Officer Wilson said.

"You shouldn't be telling her all this," Randy said, looking nervous. "Let's kill them and get out of here."

Officer Wilson shot him an annoyed look. "We can't just shoot them, you idiot. We have to make this look like a murder-suicide. Like we did with Krigbaum."

"Have you been working for Danvers since California?" Rachel asked, desperately searching for a way to keep her talking.

Officer Wilson puffed up proudly. "Yes, we have. I worked for the LAPD then, but the Feds were getting close to solving it, so we all moved to Florida and took some time off. Once Danvers bought his island, we started up again."

"Why?" Rachel asked. "Why would you want to kill innocent young women?"

The officer sneered at her. "Do you know what it's like to live on a cop's salary? It sucks. This brought in the kind of money we'd never have dreamt of." She turned to Amber. "But you had to go and ruin everything by running away after getting a good look at Krigbaum." Officer Wilson grinned evilly. "So, I think Amber should have to watch her friends die first before she kills herself. Everyone will think the poor girl snapped and couldn't live with her kidnapping memories anymore."

Rachel stood, waving the girls to move toward the end of the sofa. "No one is going to die today," she said. "Jack and I knew it was you, and you'll be caught immediately."

Officer Wilson laughed. "You knew no such thing. Your cop friend is as much in the dark as that stupid Agent Carver."

As Officer Wilson laughed, Rachel waved for the girls to go. "Run!" she yelled. They got up and sprinted down the hallway into Jules' room, locking the door behind them.

"Get them, you idiot!" Officer Wilson screamed at Randy. At that moment, a crash came from the back of the house, and by the time Randy made it to the hallway, Captain ran toward him, leaping up and grabbing his arm in his jaws.

Officer Wilson looked toward the dog for one second, and Rachel took her chance. She picked up a driftwood sculpture from her coffee table and hit Officer Wilson's gun out of her hands.

As Randy screamed in pain and Officer Wilson lunged for her gun, the front door pushed open, and Jack, Agent Carver, and a whole squad of Tallahassee's finest rushed into the room. Officer Wilson almost got her gun, but it was kicked away by Jack. The other police officers ran to grab Randy and disarm him.

"Call off your dog!" Randy yelled, his arm bloody from Captain's fangs.

"Captain, release!" Jack called. Captain immediately let go and went and sat down innocently next to his owner.

Rachel ran to Jack and wrapped her arms around him. She was so relieved, she was crying. "How did you know?" she asked through her tears.

"Your phone was on the entire time," Jack said. "We heard everything."

"Let's get rid of the trash, and we'll fill you in later," Agent Carver said as the police officers hauled away Wilson and Randy. "I have to make a call to grab Danvers, so he doesn't get on a plane and head for his island." Agent Carver pulled out his phone as he left the room.

"The girls!" Rachel pulled away from Jack. She turned to go get them, but Jules and Amber were already running down the hallway. There were tears all around as they hugged each other. They had been moments from death, and now they were safe.

After hugging the girls, Rachel walked over to Captain and kneeled in front of the large dog. "Thank you for saving us," she said, wrapping her arms around Captain. The dog laid his head on her shoulder.

"He was the hero of the day," Jules said, walking over to pet the dog. Amber did, also.

"Hey. I brought the FBI and the police. Aren't I a hero?" Jack teased.

"You got your hug," Rachel said, smiling. "But this boy literally crashed through my screen door to save us."

Jack laughed. "I knew he'd be helpful." He glanced around and picked up Rachel's phone from the floor. "I guess we can turn this off now."

She smiled. "It was Wilson who knocked it out of my hands. She had no idea it was still on."

"She wasn't as smart as she thought," Jack said, grinning.

"No, she wasn't, thank goodness," Rachel said.

"I think we all need a glass of wine." Jack headed for the refrigerator.

"I'm going to call my parents and tell them it's over," Amber said. "They'll feel so much better."

"We all feel better," Rachel said.

They sat at the counter, and each sipped a glass of red wine. Amber told her parents the happy news, and they were ecstatic. Finally, they could relax about their daughter being in Tallahassee.

Agent Carver knocked on the front door and walked in. "They're off to jail, and Danvers has been picked up," he announced. "I said to let them all stew in a cell for a while." He looked at their glasses of wine. "You wouldn't have a beer, would you?" he asked. "I could really go for one."

Rachel laughed. "Yes, we do." She grabbed a bottle out of the refrigerator and offered him a glass, but he shook his head no. "Bottle's fine."

Rachel sat down and looked from Jack to Agent Carver. "At what point did you two decide you needed to come here?"

"The moment I saw you weren't at the police station, I started asking questions," Jack said. "I knew you'd show up on time. The officer behind the desk said Officer Wilson wasn't due back for any appointments. Agent Carver showed up, and we both had a bad feeling. When I called and heard Wilson's voice, I knew we had to get here fast."

"And we did," Agent Carver said. "Jack ran every red light. It was a good thing we brought the entire police force with us." He chuckled. "He'd also shown me the airport video. It was proof that Krigbaum was bringing the women to the plane, and Danvers was in on it too. They were both so stupid to be caught on video."

"So, you believed us?" Rachel asked.

"I did then. And I never trusted Wilson. She was always trying to insert herself in the case. That night we had the first search for Amber, Wilson wasn't even supposed to be heading the search. The FBI was in charge. Now we know she just wanted to find Amber before anyone else did."

Jack handed Rachel his phone with the incriminating airport video. One of the victims, Jennifer Collins, had somehow escaped from the hangar and tried to run, but Krigbaum and Danvers caught her and brought her back to the plane.

"Wow," Rachel said, feeling intensely sad for the young woman. "It's great evidence, but just imagine how scared she was."

"I can imagine," Amber said. "I'm glad she at least tried."

Rachel gently placed her hand on Amber's arm. "I know you understand. I'm so happy you succeeded."

"We'll be sure to go through the rest of the airport video," Agent Carver said. "Anything we can pin on them will help. And then there's the black van and any DNA we can find."

Jack spoke up. "My office has gone through it with a fine-tooth comb. We'll send it off to you ASAP. The more victims we can connect to that van, the better."

Agent Carver shook his head. "I know you two thought I didn't believe you, but I did. The problem was I couldn't prove anything against Danvers. That's why I stayed close to him. I knew he was guilty as hell in California, but he got away. I just had to find the right evidence against him here."

"Officer Wilson sure surprised me," Rachel said, taking a sip of her wine. "But now that I know she was involved, I can see all the signs pointing to her. She was the only person I told that Amber was at her parents' house, and then their house was broken into. I'd also given Wilson the video of Krigbaum trying to break into my house. The next day, he was dead."

"Interesting," Agent Carver said. "Be sure to write all that down. Every bit of evidence helps." He drank the last sip of his beer and stood. "Thanks. I needed that. Now, I'm off to interrogate the murderers. Let's hope one of them sings."

Jack stood and shook his hand. "Thanks for putting up with us. I know we drove you crazy, but it all worked out in the end."

"It did," Agent Carver said. "I'll let you know what happens." He walked out the front door to his car.

Jack set his wine glass in the sink. "I think I have a screen door to fix."

Rachel laughed. "That can wait. We've just solved a big case. Let's relax and let that sink in."

"Gladly," Jack said, sitting down again. Everyone laughed.

CHAPTER SIXTEEN

Over the next few days, Jack and Rachel were busy giving their statements to the police. As Agent Carver had hoped, Officer Wilson sang like a bird. She told them Johnathan Danvers was the ringleader and Krigbaum had done all the murders. No plea deal was in the works yet for her cooperation because they were still collecting evidence. Rachel hoped that Wilson spent decades in jail for orchestrating the abduction and murder of so many young women.

Rachel had told Avery everything that had happened once she got a minute to herself. He was upset that she'd been in danger but glad they were all safe now.

"I hope they can tie all those murders to them and put them away for good," Avery said. "Rich people tend to get away with murder."

"Not this time. Officer Wilson gave so many details on Danvers' involvement, I don't think he'll be able to con his way out of it," Rachel told him. "Imagine. He had everything money could buy, and still, it wasn't enough. He thought he was above everyone."

"Thank goodness he was caught. And hopefully, we'll catch our guy, too. I tell you, these cases can get depressing over time," Avery said.

"Then we need to take off at some point and go somewhere quiet. Just you and I," Rachel said.

"I like that idea. Be sure to tell Jack I appreciate everything he's done for you and the girls. I'm glad he could be there," Avery said.

"Really?" Rachel teased. "You mean you aren't jealous of him anymore?"

Avery chuckled. "Well, yeah, I still am. But he's a good guy, and I appreciate his watching over you."

"And Captain, too," Rachel said.

"Definitely, Captain, too," Avery said.

Jules and Amber moved back into their apartment that week, and Rachel knew they were relieved to get on with their lives. School would start on Monday, and they were ready for it. But there was one more emotional event they had to get through before life could move on.

On Friday, Rachel, Jules, Jack, and a small group of people stood around Julie's grave as the minister said a few words and a prayer. Amber was there, too, and so was Julie's longtime caregiver, Shirley. Avery was unable to attend and had told Rachel how sorry he was to miss it. But she understood. He was doing important work, and she wanted him to continue.

"I'm so sorry, dear," Shirley said, hugging Rachel, then Jules after the minister had finished speaking. "Julie was such a kind soul. She will be missed."

"Thank you," Rachel said. "And thank you for taking such good care of her."

"Oh, darling girl. It was my pleasure," Shirley said.

They all parted ways after that. Jack and Rachel had ridden together, so he drove her home.

"I can stay a couple more days," Jack said once they were at the house. "I'd hate to think of you being here alone after everything."

She smiled at him. Jack was such a nice guy, and while she would have loved having the company, she'd taken up too much of his time already. "That's very kind of you, but you have a life and a job to get back to. And you also need to work on solving the murder case of the young woman in Panama City Beach."

"It all can wait," he said. "We're waiting on the DNA samples and comparisons, and that will take a while. The most important thing right now is you."

Rachel walked over and wrapped her arms around Jack. "I appreciate everything you've done for me and Amber these past couple of weeks. You're a true friend."

Jack pulled away slightly but still held her. "Friend, huh?"

Rachel felt bad. She truly liked Jack, but she was already in a relationship. "I'm sorry, but that's the way it has to be. Avery and I are a couple."

Jack nodded. "I know. But you can't blame a guy for trying." He hugged her close again, then let go. "So, you want me to ship out?"

Rachel laughed. "Go home. Relax. Take Captain out for a run on the beach. You both deserve a quiet weekend after everything that's happened."

"Okay," Jack said. "But I'm sure it won't be long before you need help again." He grinned.

"What? Do you think I'm that helpless?" she asked.

"No. I think you're a magnet for murder cases. It won't be

long, and you'll be calling me."

This made Rachel laugh doubly hard. "I certainly hope not. The last thing anyone wants is to be involved with a murder."

"Uh, huh," Jack said. "We'll see."

-End-

ABOUT THE AUTHOR

Deanna Lynn Sletten loves a good murder mystery. As a child, she was fascinated by her great-uncle's job as a forensic scientist for the Los Angeles County Sheriff's Department. Her first chapter books were *Nancy Drew Mysteries,* and she could never say no to an Agatha Christie novel. It's also not surprising that she loves watching true-crime stories on television. So, it was only a matter of time that Deanna would try her hand at writing a murder mystery.

Deanna has been writing novels since 2011 and is always up for a challenge. She writes women's fiction, romance, historical fiction, and now murder mysteries. She lives in northern Minnesota with her husband and has two grown children. Her favorite thing to do is walk the wooded trails around her home with her adorable Aussie.

Learn more at: DeannaLSletten.com

www.ingramcontent.com/pod-product-compliance
Lightning Source LLC
Chambersburg PA
CBHW051243170626
46809CB00004B/1465